SHIRLEY & JAMILA'S BIG FALL

by Gillian Goerz

Dial Books for Young Readers

DIAL BOOKS FOR YOUNG READERS
An imprint of Penguin Random House LLC, New York

First published in the United States of America by Dial Books for Young Readers,
an imprint of Penguin Random House LLC, 2021

Visit us online at penguinrandomhouse.com.

Library of Congress Cataloging-in-Publication Data
Names: Goerz, Gillian, author, illustrator. Title: Shirley & Jamila's big fall / Gillian Goerz.
Other titles: Shirley and Jamila's big fall | Description: New York : Dial Books for Young Readers, an imprint of Penguin Random House LLC, 2021. | Audience: Ages 8–12. | Audience: Grades 4–6. | Summary: Starting a new school in the fall with her friend Shirley, everything is going well for Jamila until Shirley pulls her into a new assignment: stop Chuck Milton, a school bully who is using blackmail and intimidation to become school president—an assignment that will involve a bit of breaking and entering. | Identifiers: LCCN 2021015245 (print) | LCCN 2021015246 (ebook) | ISBN 9780525552888 (hardcover) | ISBN 9780525552895 (paperback) | ISBN 9780593405413 (ebook) | ISBN 9780593405406 (ebook) | ISBN 9780525552901 (ebook) | Subjects: LCSH: Best friends—Comic books, strips, etc. | Best friends—Juvenile fiction. | Schools—Comic books, strips, etc. | Schools—Juvenile fiction. | Bullying—Juvenile fiction. | Bullying—Juvenile fiction. | Extortion—Comic books, strips, etc. | Extortion—Juvenile fiction. | Graphic novels. | CYAC: Graphic novels. | Best friends—Fiction. | Friendship—Fiction. | School—Fiction. | Bullying—Fiction. | Extortion—Fiction. | LCGFT: Graphic novels.
Classification: LCC PZ7.7.G6533 Sj 2021 (print) | LCC PZ7.7.G6533 (ebook) | DDC 741.5/973—dc23
LC record available at https://lccn.loc.gov/2021015245 | LC ebook record available at https://lccn.loc.gov/2021015246

Manufactured in China
ISBN 9780525552895 (pbk) 10 9 8 7 6 5 4 3 2 1
ISBN 9780525552888 (hc) 10 9 8 7 6 5 4 3 2 1
RRD

Design by Jennifer Kelly and Gillian Goerz
Text set in GG Sans with permission of the author

Produced with the support of the Ontario Arts Council.

FOR RAMONA QUIMBY.
YOU'RE MY FAVORITE, EVEN THOUGH
YOU'RE PRETEND. ALSO FOR THE LATE
BEVERLY CLEARY, WHO INTRODUCED US
AND IN DOING SO, IN A VERY SLOW WAY,
MADE THIS BOOK HAPPEN.

Prologue
THE DAY BEFORE THE FIRST DAY OF SCHOOL.
Yorkv

BOYS
GIRLS
BACK TO SCHOOL
FITTING ROOMS

wonder Child

GOT 'EM
BACK TO SCHOOL LIST
GRADE FIVE

ZZZZZZZ

JAMILA!
THAT'S ME.

THAT'S MY BEST FRIEND.
SHIRLEY!

SHIRLEY BONES:
Are you ready?

JAMILA WAHEED:
Do I have a choice?
JAMILA WAHEED:
Don't answer that.

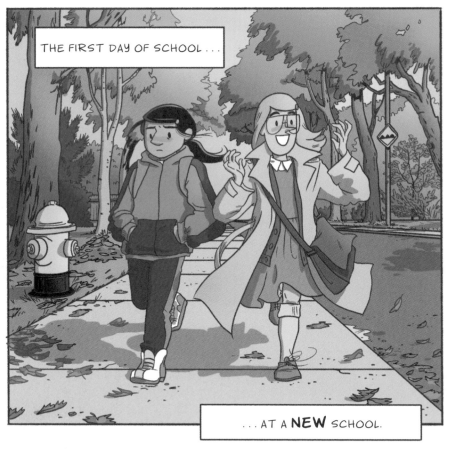

THE FIRST DAY OF SCHOOL . . .

. . . AT A **NEW** SCHOOL.

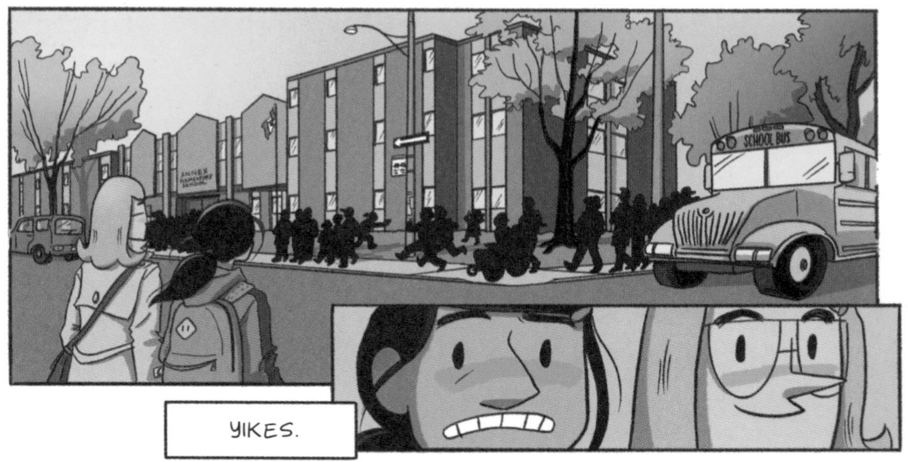

MRS. LEZAMA, THIS IS JAMILA WAHEED. SHE'S NEW.
I WAS EXPECTING YOU! SO GLAD YOU'RE HERE!
MY TEACHER WAS NICE. AND HAVING A FRIEND THERE ALREADY SURE HELPED.

BY THE TIME A WEEK HAD PASSED, I FORGOT I'D BEEN NERVOUS AT ALL.

BASKETBALL TRY OUTS
THE WILD WORLD OF
STUDENT
LUNCH CLUB

IN A WAY, IT WASN'T THAT DIFFERENT FROM OUR SUMMER.
ANNEX ELEMENTARY
IT EVEN FELT FAMILIAR.

Chapter 1
SWISH
SCHOOL WAS WELL UNDERWAY WHEN THE STORY I'M ABOUT TO TELL TOOK PLACE.

I WOULDN'T BE TELLING IT NOW IF THE KIDS INVOLVED COULD STILL BE HURT (OR GET IN TROUBLE) BY THE TRUTH COMING OUT, BUT THEY'VE ALL MOVED AWAY OR MOVED ON.

STILL, IF I FUDGE A DETAIL OR TWO JUST TO MAKE SURE, I HOPE YOU'LL UNDERSTAND.
LIKE I SAID, AT FIRST SCHOOL DIDN'T CHANGE THINGS THAT MUCH FOR SHIRLEY AND ME.

WE SOLVED CASES TOGETHER.
WE HELPED KIDS OUT.
WE EVEN SNUCK AROUND A LITTLE.

KENNY-BABY
Have a super day!
Love Mommy

IT WAS GREAT.
TEACHER'S LOUNGE

BUT SUDDENLY, THERE WAS OTHER STUFF TOO.

THERE WERE VIOLIN LESSONS.

THERE WAS BASKETBALL.
NEW COMERS WELCOM
I MADE THE SCHOOL TEAM **AND** A COMMUNITY TEAM.

THERE WAS HOMEWORK.
TRUE CRIME
MURDER! CRIME!

RRRIIINNNGGGG
THERE WERE ALSO OTHER KIDS.

IN SUMMER, SHIRLEY AND I SPENT ALMOST EVERY DAY TOGETHER.

REC CENTER

NOW WE WERE BUSIER.

COMMUNITY
RECREATION
CENTRE
MY COMMUNITY BASKETBALL TEAM PRACTICED AT THE NEARBY REC CENTER AFTER SCHOOL A FEW DAYS A WEEK.

EXIT
COMMUNITY
GIRLS LEAGUE
PRACTICE
TODAY!
DRY ERASE

EXIT
LEX
LITA
MADDY
ALICE
LILAH
AUDREY
NANCY
SEENA

SEENA WAS THE FIRST REAL FRIEND I MADE AFTER SHIRLEY.

I WENT TO COMMUNITY LEAGUE TRYOUTS BY MYSELF.
TRY OUTS
I DIDN'T SEE ANYONE FROM MY CLASS.

HAVE YOU DONE THESE NEIGHBORHOOD LEAGUES BEFORE?
HM?

DID YOU PLAY ON THIS TEAM LAST YEAR?
NO, I JUST MOVED HERE IN SUMMER. DID YOU?

IF I HAD, I WOULDN'T HAVE HAD TO ASK YOU.

RIGHT.
BASIC DEDUCTION.
I'M TEASING. IT'S MY FIRST TIME ON THIS TEAM TOO. I GO TO PALMERSTON SCHOOL. ARE YOU AT ANNEX ELEMENTARY?

YUP. JUST STARTED. WHAT POSITION DO YOU PLAY?
POINT GUARD. ALL THE WAY. YOU?

SHOOTING GUARD OR SMALL FORWARD? I'M NOT SURE. I MOSTLY PLAY WITH MY OLDER BROTHER OR BY MYSELF.
YOUR BROTHER PLAYS BALL?

YEAH, FAROOQ PLAYS ON HIS HIGH SCHOOL TEAM.
WHOA. THAT'S LUCKY. MY OLDER SISTER DOESN'T PLAY SPORTS. SHE'S COOL, THOUGH.

YOUR BROTHER'S NAME'S *FAROOQ?* WHAT'S *YOUR* NAME?
JAMILA. WHAT'S YOURS?

I'M SEENA. HASEENA, REALLY. BUT ONLY TO MY MOM.

ARE YOU PAKISTANI? I HAVE AN UNCLE FAROOQ ON MY DAD'S SIDE.

MY PARENTS CAME FROM PAKISTAN, BUT I WAS BORN HERE. IS YOUR UNCLE FAROOQ A SIXTEEN-YEAR-OLD GOOF-OFF WHO LIVES AT MY HOUSE? BECAUSE IF HE IS, WE ARE RELATED.

AUNTY JAMILA?!
YES, BHANJI! IT IS, I, YOUR AUNTY. I'M VERY DISAPPOINTED IN HOW MUCH TIME YOU PLAY BASKETBALL.

OH AUNTY! IT'S JUST YOUR EYESIGHT! I'M NOT EVEN PLAYING BALL! I'M STUDYING RIGHT NOW!
WHERE ARE YOU? I CAN'T SEE! FIND MY GLASSES!

HA
HA HA HA
HAHAHAHA
WHERE ARE SEENA AND JAMILA? YOU'RE UP NEXT!

THAT'S US!
HERE! WE'RE HERE!
SEENA WAS FUNNY.

SEENA WAS **GOOD** TOO.
WE BOTH MADE THE TEAM, NO PROBLEM.

COACH TRIED ME ON DIFFERENT POSITIONS, WHICH WAS FUN AND KIND OF SCARY. I'D NEVER PLAYED ON A BIG TEAM BEFORE.

SEENA WAS A POINT GUARD ALL RIGHT.
THAT'S SORT OF THE LEADERSHIP POSITION.

THEY DRIVE THE PLAYS. THEY PASS A LOT—NO BALL-HOGS—AND THEY GOTTA REALLY HOLLER AT EVERYONE TO KEEP TRACK OF WHO'S WHERE.

SEENA WAS GREAT AT ALL OF IT.

RIGHT AWAY, EVERYONE WAS KIND OF IN AWE OF HER.
ME INCLUDED.

BUT IT TURNED OUT SEENA AND I HAD SO MUCH IN COMMON.

MY MOM REALLY LIKED YOUR MOM.
REALLY? SHE CAN BE PRETTY TOUGH.

SHE SAID YOUR MOM IS REALLY FUNNY.

ARE YOU SERIOUS?

UH-HUH.

I GUESS SHE'S KINDA FUNNY . . .

HER MOM'S AFGHAN AND HER DAD'S PAKISTANI, SO WHEN *MY* MOM INSISTED ON CALLING **AND** MEETING IN PERSON BEFORE I COULD COME OVER, SEENA TOTALLY GOT IT. HER PARENTS HAD INSISTED ON THE SAME THING THEMSELVES.

MY MOM'S PRETTY WEIRD, SO IF SHE LIKES YOUR MOM, I BET *SHE'S* WEIRD TOO.
"WEIRD." WHEN SEENA SAID IT, I WONDERED WHAT SHE MEANT.

MY FAMILY LIVED IN AN APARTMENT BEFORE . . .

BUT IT WASN'T LIKE THIS.

THIS IS TAZI.
HE'S AN OLD RAT.
HE'S A *RAT*?

HA! NO, HE'S JUST A RATTY OLD DOG THAT LIKES A GOOD SMASH. COME ON! GIVE HIM A SMASHY-SMASH.

PAT

GO ON.
SMASH.

OH, TAZI'S IN HEAVEN NOW.

MOHR! I THOUGHT YOU WERE STILL AT WORK.

I DECIDED TO WORK FROM HOME TODAY, BABYLOVE.
MOOOOHR!

YOU MUST BE JAMILA!
YEAH, MOHR! JAMILA! JAMILA!

NICE TO MEET YOU, MRS.—
OH, CALL ME AISHA! EYE-SHA, NOT EYE-EE-SHA —YOU GET IT.
PEOPLE ALWAYS GET IT WRONG.

I GET "JUH-MILL-UH" SOMETIMES.
HOW DARE THEY?! JA-MEE-LA IS PERFECTION! IT'S A FANTASTIC NAME AND SUITS YOU TO A TEE, MY DARLING!

OUR MOMS MIGHT LIKE EACH OTHER, BUT THEY'RE VERY DIFFERENT.
AMMI WOULD **NEVER** LET ME DO THIS TO MY ROOM.
IF SEENA'S MOM WAS WEIRD, THEN WEIRD WAS GREAT.

WE PLAYED VIDEO GAMES! (THE SYSTEM WAS OLD AND WE HAD A TIME LIMIT, BUT STILL!)
AISHA BROUGHT US SALTED RADISHES AND CHILI CHEESE TOAST TO EAT **IN SEENA'S ROOM**!

SEENA'S DAD, WHO SAID TO CALL HIM **SAMEER,** IS A REAL ARTIST AND HE BROUGHT HOME ALL OF THIS KIMCHI AND THEY LET ME CHOP WITH THE BIG KNIFE.

SEENA'S SISTER, NOOR, WAS REALLY FUNNY. SHE WANTS TO MAKE MOVIES LIKE AISHA WHO ALSO DOES SOMETHING CALLED "FILM PROGRAMMING" . . .
IT WAS ONE OF MY FAVORITE DINNERS, I THINK. MAYBE EVER.

Chapter 2

I EXPECTED YOU FROM THE OTHER DOOR. WHAT PERCENTAGE TAKE THE DOOR TO THE FIELD, AS OPPOSED TO THE ONE INTO THE HALLWAY? WHAT FACTORS INFLUENCE THAT?

UH . . . I BETTER STICK AROUND HERE. MAYBE ANOTHER DAY?
OH-KAY. YOU DO YOU. SEE YOU NEXT PRACTICE.

SO, WHERE ARE WE HEADED?
HAVE A LOOK.
CHUCK
The time works. Rec center, green picnic table.
Donezo.
I DON'T KNOW CHUCK.
YOU'RE NEW. IF YOU'D BEEN HERE ANY LONGER, YOU'D HAVE HEARD OF THIS KID.
IF YOU GET A SHIVER LIKE SPIDERS ARE WALKING OVER YOU AS YOU SLEEP, IT PROBABLY MEANS **CHUCK MILTON** IS NEARBY.
I'VE MET MY SHARE OF SNEAKY CREEPS...
BUT NO SNEAK CREEPS ME OUT LIKE HIM.

I'D AVOID HIM IF I COULD, BUT TODAY I ACTUALLY ASKED **HIM** TO MEET **ME**.

< CHUCK
I need to talk: pick a time. —Shirley Bones for E.
Tomorrow after some Presidential Business. 5 pm. Where?

SO WHO IS HE? WHAT GRADE IS HE IN? DOES HE GO HERE? WHAT'S THIS ALL ABOUT?
THOSE ARE THE REAL QUESTIONS.

I'LL TELL YOU QUICKLY BEFORE HE ARRIVES.

CHUCK MILTON IS IN GRADE SIX—CLASS PRESIDENT, ACTUALLY, HERE AT OUR SCHOOL—AND HE'S VICIOUS BY DESIGN.
HE BUYS HIS CANDY AND COLLECTABLES WITH THE MISERY OF OTHERS.
HE'S VERY SMART—I WON'T PRETEND HE HASN'T DONE SOMETHING INTELLIGENT.
IF HE WOULD PUT HIS MIND TO SOMETHING **GOOD**, HE'D PROBABLY BE BRILLIANT.
INSTEAD HE BUYS AND SELLS **SECRETS**.

EVERYONE IN SCHOOL KNOWS THAT IF YOU HAVE DIRT ON SOMEONE ELSE
—AND WAHEED, TRUST ME WHEN I SAY NOTHING IS OFF LIMITS—
CHUCK WILL BUY IT FROM YOU.
send
CHOCOLATE BARS, CHEAT CODES, EVEN ACTUAL CASH— HE'LL PAY IT TO WHOEVER HAS TANGIBLE BLACKMAIL ON SOMEONE ELSE.
Super Choc
5
secret.mov
send
ELECTR Games
PHOTOS, LETTERS, SCREENGRABS, FORGED PERMISSION SLIPS . . . BUT **NOTHING FAKE.** HE'S "LEGIT" IN HIS WAY.

AVERY LEE TRIED TO PASS OFF A PHOTOSHOPPED PICTURE AND BOY, DID HE REGRET IT.
CHUCK FOUND OUT AND OFFERED TRIPLE FOR DIRT ON *AVERY.*
IN THE END, AVERY WAS KICKED OFF THE DODGEBALL TEAM AND GOT GROUNDED FOR A MONTH.

CHUCK HELD ON TO A JUICY NOTE FOR A WHOLE YEAR JUST TO SAVE IT FOR THE WEEK BEFORE THE SCHOOL PLAY.
ROBIN HOOD

IF IT WOULD HAVE GOT OUT, IRIS ACOSTA—YOU DON'T KNOW HER—WOULD HAVE LOST THE LEAD ROLE.

HE COULD ASK ANY PRICE HE WANTED.

YOU CAN BET SHE PAID.

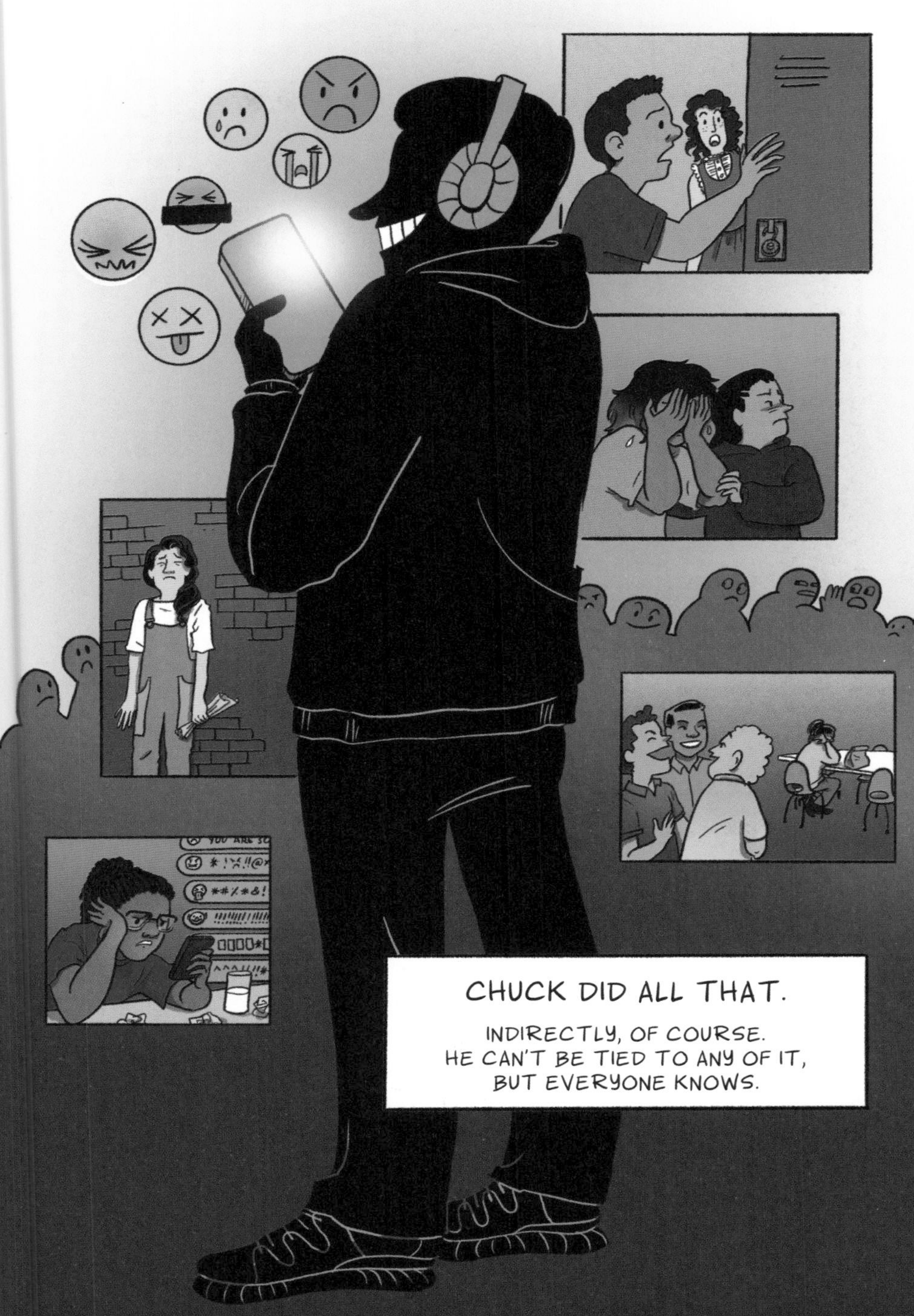
CHUCK DID ALL THAT.
INDIRECTLY, OF COURSE.
HE CAN'T BE TIED TO ANY OF IT,
BUT EVERYONE KNOWS.

THERE ARE BULLIES AND JERKS THAT WILL TRIP YOU AND STEAL YOUR LUNCH WITHOUT THINKING TWICE, BUT IT'S A SPECIAL KIND OF KID WHO TORTURES OTHER KIDS FOR THE FUN OF IT—WHILE THE TEACHERS GIVE HIM STRAIGHT A'S.

SHIRLEY DIDN'T GET THIS FIRED UP VERY OFTEN.

AND NO ONE TELLS ON HIM?

THEY WOULDN'T DARE.

HE ONLY BUYS REAL DIRT THAT KIDS DO NOT WANT OUT THERE. WHO CARES IF HE GETS A WEEK OF DETENTION IF EVERYONE STILL FINDS OUT YOU PEED YOUR PANTS ON THE SCHOOL TRIP?

HE DOESN'T ATTACK PEOPLE WITH NOTHING TO HIDE. EVERYONE ON HIS LIST HAS A REAL SECRET, SO HE HAS ALL THE POWER.

SO WHY ARE WE MEETING HIM?

BECAUSE MY—**OUR** NEW CLIENT, IF YOU WILL . . .
I WILL.
NOD
. . . HAS ASKED FOR HELP.

DO YOU KNOW EVA MAKWA? SHE'S IN GRADE SIX WITH CHUCK, AND A SENSITIVE NOTE OF HERS HAS FALLEN INTO HIS HANDS.

I TRUST HER AND SHE ASSURES ME THIS NOTE COULD MAKE SCHOOL A NIGHTMARE FOR HER.

CHUCK WILL SPILL THE BEANS IF EVA DOESN'T PAY UP. SHE'S SCRAMBLING TO BABYSIT AND BORROW, BUT SHE CAN'T GET ENOUGH.

SHE'S ASKED ME TO TALK TO HIM, AND SEE IF HE'LL ACCEPT WHAT SHE'S GOT.

IS THAT HIM?

SNAP

CHOMP

CANDY UPDATE
BUBBLE TAPE:
A FOOT OR MORE OF ROLLED UP FLAT GUM. GREAT FOR SHARING. HYPOTHETICALLY.

POP

SORRY I'M A BIT LATE. I HAD A TEXT THAT ABSOLUTELY DEMANDED MY ATTENTION.
HE TALKED LIKE HE WAS A LAWYER OR SOME KIND OF RICH GROWN-UP ON TV. AND DRESSED LIKE WE'RE IN PRIVATE SCHOOL.

SHIRLEY? I'M CHARLES, BUT YOU KNOW THE KIDS HERE USUALLY CALL ME CHUCK AND WHO AM I TO SAY NO? HAHAHA

IN FRONT OF HER? SHE CAN KEEP A SECRET?
JAMILA WORKS WITH ME.

WELL, IF **YOU** THINK IT'S OKAY. IT'S A VERY **PRIVATE** MATTER AFTER ALL. **SENSITIVE** INFORMATION. THINGS YOU WOULDN'T WANT GETTING **AROUND** . . .
JAMILA'S GOOD.

FINE. THEN LET'S TALK. YOU SAID YOU'RE HERE IN OUR DEAR LITTLE FRIEND EVA'S PLACE. HAS SHE AGREED TO MY OFFER?

LET'S REVIEW THIS OFFER.
IN EXCHANGE FOR HER LITTLE **NOTE** . . . $400 IN CASH.

WHAT! HOW'S A KID SUPPOSED TO GET THAT MUCH MONEY?

IT IS A LOT OF MONEY FOR A KID. IF EVA FAILS?
AW, THAT KIND OF NEGATIVITY REALLY GETS ME DOWN.
I, FOR ONE, THINK EVA IS A TOTAL ROCK STAR WHO CAN DO ANYTHING SHE SETS HER MIND TO.
I STAY POSITIVE...
WHICH IS WHY I DON'T LIKE TO THINK ABOUT WHAT WOULD HAPPEN IF SHE HAD TO DEAL WITH THE GOSSIP SHARKS AT THIS SCHOOL.
CHILDREN CAN BE SO CRUEL.
YOU ACT LIKE YOU KNOW EXACTLY WHAT WILL HAPPEN.
I WILL ADVISE MY CLIENT TO CONFESS! SHE WILL CONTROL THE STORY AND TRUST THAT "CHILDREN" ARE NOT AS HORRIBLE AS YOU SEEM TO THINK.

HMM-HMM-HMM-
HMM-HMM-
THAT CHUCKLE.
QUIET AND HORRIBLE.
OH, SHIRLEY,
SHIRLEY.
SHIRLEY, SHIRLEY,
SHIRLEY —
STOP.
ARE YOU OKAY?
YOU SEEM
AGITATED.

YOU KNOW, **SHIRLEY**, YOU HAVE A REPUTATION FOR BEING SMARTER THAN THIS.

THE INFORMATION IN THIS NOTE IS **NOT** SOMETHING THAT WILL BLOW OVER **QUICKLY**. REMEMBER WHAT HAPPENED TO THE POOR LITTLE STUDENT COUNCIL PRESIDENT LAST YEAR? KIDS WERE **VERY** INTERESTED IN HER STORY. DOES SHE EVEN GO HERE ANYMORE? HMMM. NO, AS A MATTER OF FACT, SHE CHANGED SCHOOLS.

EVA'S CLASSMATES WILL FIND HER NOTE **VERY INTERESTING.**

I SUSPECT THEY AREN'T THE ONLY ONES.

THIS INFORMATION WILL FOLLOW EVERYONE INVOLVED FOR THE REST OF THE YEAR . . .

PERHAPS EVEN INTO HIGH SCHOOL AND BEYOND.

WITH A LITTLE HELP.

BUT IT'S ALL THE SAME TO ME! IF YOU TRUST THE KIND HEARTS OF THE STUDENTS OF THIS SCHOOL, THE GENEROSITY OF SPIRIT OF ALL THE PEOPLE INVOLVED, THEN OF COURSE IT WOULD BE SILLY TO SPEND SO MUCH TO GET ONE LITTLE NOTE BACK!

BY ALL MEANS, ADVISE YOUR CLIENT!

SHRUG

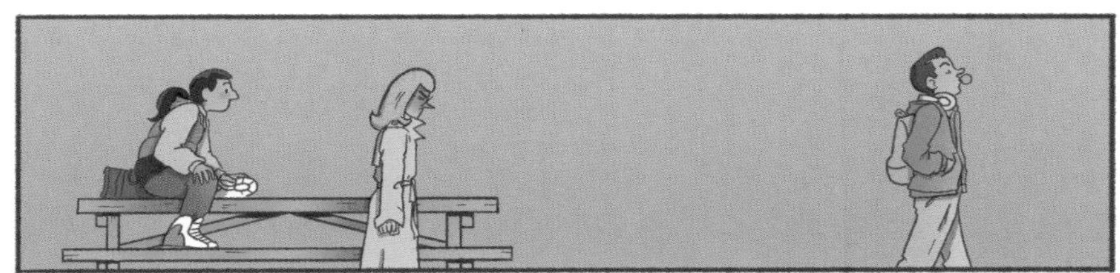

WAIT.

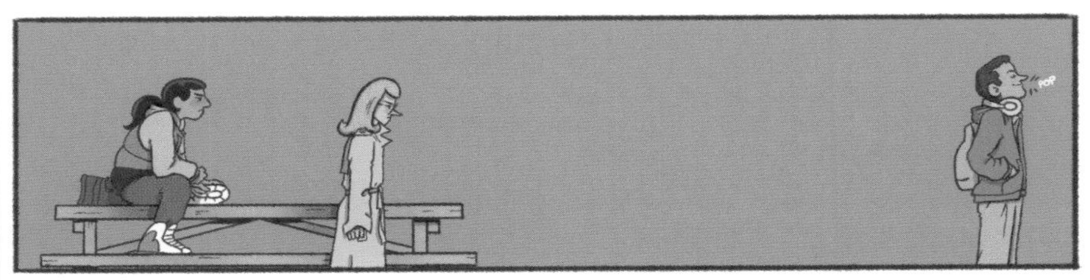
POP

NO NEED TO RACE OFF. WE AGREE IT IS A CAREFUL ISSUE. THAT SHOULD BE TREATED CAREFULLY.

I'M SO GLAD YOU AGREE. I THOUGHT YOU MIGHT.
STILL . . . EVA ISN'T RICH. SHE HAS GATHERED $150—AN IMPRESSIVE AMOUNT—IN A VERY IMPRESSIVE AMOUNT OF TIME, BY USING EVERY FAVOR SHE HAS, AND SAVING EVERY PENNY SHE HAS TO HER NAME.

$400 IS IMPOSSIBLE. BE PRACTICAL. ACCEPT $150 IN EXCHANGE FOR THE NOTE. IT'S THE MOST YOU CAN POSSIBLY GET FROM HER.
I KNOW ALL OF THIS. ABOUT HER FINANCIALS, HER EFFORTS TO RAISE THE MONEY.

BUT YOU HAVE TO ADMIT, WITH THE ART STREAM INTERVIEW AROUND THE CORNER, IT'S A PERFECT TIME FOR HER BEST FRIENDS AND LOVED ONES TO HELP OUT. TO MAKE SURE SHE SUCCEEDS.
THE ART STREAM?
THERE'S AN ADVANCED ART PROGRAM HERE THAT GRADE SIXES APPLY FOR.

IF YOU DON'T GET IN FOR GRADE SEVEN, THAT'S IT.
WHICH IS WHY EVA NEEDS TO PRIORITIZE.
MY CLIENT **HAS** PRIORITIZED. SHE'S ALREADY OFFERING YOU MUCH MORE THAN SHE CAN AFFORD. WHAT YOU'RE ASKING IS IMPOSSIBLE AND YOU KNOW IT.
IT'S SMARTER TO TAKE THE $150 THAN SAY NO AND GET NOTHING!
OOOH, I **THINK** THAT'S A SLIIIIIIGHT MISCALCULATION, MISS **BONES.**
I HAVE SEVERAL SIMILAR CASES SIMMERING AS WE SPEAK. IN FACT, ON MY WAY TO MEET YOU, I RECEIVED NOT ONE BUT TWO VERY PROMISING, AND VERIFIED, ATTACHMENTS.
IF EVA'S SECRET WERE EXPOSED, I THINK HER EXAMPLE WOULD MOTIVATE **MANY** OF MY **DEAR LITTLE FRIENDS** TO COOPERATE, DON'T YOU?

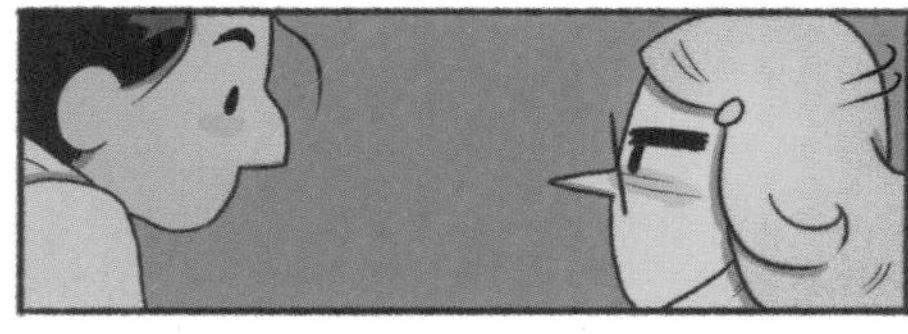

JAMILA! GRAB HIS PHONE! I'VE GOT HIS BACKPACK!

GIRLS, GIRLS. HONESTLY, I EXPECTED BETTER FROM YOU, ESPECIALLY SHIRLEY BONES, "FAMOUS GIRL DETECTIVE."
JUST "DETECTIVE" WILL DO.

WILL IT?
'CUZ KIDS STUPIDER THAN YOU, WITH NO REPUTATIONS, NO IMAGINARY TITLES, HAVE TRIED THE SAME THING, AND BLEW IT JUST AS BADLY AS YOU'RE BLOWING IT NOW.

DO YOU THINK I JUST CARRY THIS STUFF AROUND? TO **SCHOOL**? HERE IN THIS **BACKPACK** THAT ANYONE COULD JUST GET THEIR HANDS ON?
SPOILER: I DON'T.
EVEN IF YOU **COULD** UNLOCK MY PHONE (YOU CAN'T), I'M IN THE CLOUD, BABY!
HAHAHA! PASSWORDS ON PASSWORDS, FRIENDOS!

BESIDES, IF I WERE TO CALL THE TEACHERS OVER, AND HAPPENED TO MENTION THAT YOU STOLE MY BACKPACK AND PHONE, WHO DO YOU THINK WOULD GET IN TROUBLE?

OR BE BELIEVED?

THIS HAS BEEN FUN BUT I GOTTA GO.

GONNA VISIT A FEW **DEAR LITTLE FRIENDS** ON MY WAY HOME.

PLUCK

YANK

CAN'T WAIT TO
HEAR FROM EVA!

I'D LEARNED BY THEN TO LEAVE SHIRLEY ALONE WHEN SHE GETS *THAT LOOK.*

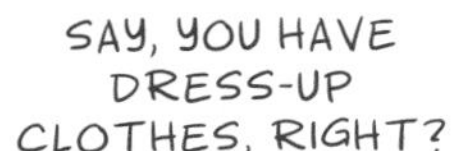
SAY, YOU HAVE DRESS-UP CLOTHES, RIGHT?

UH, YEAH. THERE'S A BOX OF OLD SHIRTS AND HATS PLUS SOME DRESSES 'N' THINGS MY MOM GOT ME THAT I NEVER WEAR.
YOU WANT TO PLAY DRESS-UP?

YES.

SHIRLEY WAS LIKE THAT. OBSESSED ONE MINUTE, TOTALLY FORGETTING THE NEXT. WE SPENT THE REST OF THE AFTERNOON GOOFING OFF IN COSTUMES.
AND IF ANY CLOTHES WERE MISSING WHEN I PACKED THEM UP AGAIN, I DIDN'T NOTICE.

Chapter 3
AFTER THAT, BASKETBALL RAMPED UP AND THE NEXT WEEK WENT BY FAST.

SEENA DID ASK ME OVER AGAIN.

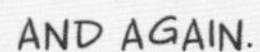
AND AGAIN.

I REALLY LIKE HOT SAUCE AND THAT MADE SAMEER SO SMILEY SOMEHOW.
NOW TRY THIS ONE! IT'S PERFECT WITH SZECHUAN!

MMMM!
BEING AT SEENA'S MADE ME SO SMILEY TOO.

WITH PRACTICES OVER NOON-HOUR AND AFTER SCHOOL, I BARELY SAW SHIRLEY OUTSIDE OF CLASS.

ROOM

IN USE

I DIDN'T KNOW WHAT SHIRLEY DID DURING THOSE PRACTICES . . .

OH, PRACTICING VIOLIN, OR WORKING ON OPEN CASES. I HAVE A FEW EXPERIMENTS ON THE GO.

I WANTED TO ASK ABOUT EVA MAKWA'S CASE,
. . .
BUT SHIRLEY HAD SEEMED SO UPSET BY CHUCK THAT I DIDN'T WANT TO BRING IT UP.

SOMETIMES THERE WERE CASES SHIRLEY COULDN'T SOLVE, AND ANYBODY WHO LIKES WINNING KNOWS IT'S NO FUN TALKING ABOUT YOUR LOSSES.

CHUCK BEAT HER, AND EACH DAY I WONDERED IF THIS WAS THE DAY WE'D HEAR SOME TERRIBLE NEWS ABOUT EVA.

AFTER COUNTLESS DAYS OF AFTER-SCHOOL PRACTICE, I FINALLY HAD AN AFTERNOON OFF AND MET UP WITH SHIRLEY TO WALK HOME TOGETHER.

YOU WOULDN'T SAY I'M ALWAYS MAKING NEW FRIENDS WOULD YOU?

HA! NO, I DON'T THINK ANYBODY WOULD.
THEN MAYBE YOU'LL BE SURPRISED TO HEAR I HAVE A BRAND-NEW FRIEND.

A BEST FRIEND.

OH.

WHAT ARE YOU TALKING ABOUT?

AS I SAID, MY BEST FRIEND GRACE MILTON—

MILTON?

LIKE CHUCK MILTON?

CHUCK MILTON'S YOUNGER SISTER, YES.

AHEM.

I'M SURE YOU KNOW THAT THE AFTER-SCHOOL BAND PROGRAM INCLUDES KIDS FROM SEVERAL DIFFERENT SCHOOLS,

AND MEETS AT THE COMMUNITY CENTER. WHERE YOUR LEAGUE PRACTICES ARE.

SAINT THERESA'S
ACADEMY FOR PRESTIGIOUS YOUNGSTERS
student identification
CLAIRE RIVERS
AGE: 10 | GRADE: 5
Claire Rivers*
SIGNATURE

IT'S VERY HANDY TO SNAP UP A VALID STUDENT ID OR TWO AS THEY GO MISSING FROM TIME TO TIME, WAHEED.

I NEVER LEAVE A LOST-AND-FOUND WITHOUT SOMETHING OF VALUE. I GOT THIS FROM THE ONE AT THE PUBLIC LIBRARY.

I GUESS YOU KINDA LOOK LIKE THIS . . .

BUT CHUCK KNOWS YOU! AND WHAT YOU LOOK LIKE! DID YOU GO TO THEIR HOUSE?

IT WAS CRITICAL THAT I GO TO THEIR HOUSE, WAHEED.
YANK
FUN FACT: CLAIRE'S FAVORITE GAME IS HIDE-AND-SEEK. I NOW KNOW THE MILTON HOUSE LIKE THE BACK OF MY HAND.

DON'T LOOK SO WORRIED.
SOMEONE LIKE CHUCK DOES NOT PAY ATTENTION TO HIS YOUNGER SISTER OR HER FRIENDS.

BESIDES, YOU DIDN'T KNOW ME TO SEE ME, SO WHY WOULD HE?
I WOULD KNOW YOU TO SEE YOU.

YOU DIDN'T THE OTHER DAY. AFTER YOUR BASKETBALL PRACTICE.
WHAT?

AUDREY, HOW COME YOU DIDN'T JOIN BAND?
MUSIC ROOM

I CAN BARELY CLAP MY HANDS TO A BEAT! BESIDES, I DON'T HAVE TIME FOR ANOTHER PRACTICE . . .
WHO HAS TIME?!
MY SISTER PLAYS FLUTE.
I HATE THE FLUTE!
YOU HATE EVERYTHING.
HA HA HA
HA! YOU DO.

THUD
AAAAAH!
WHOA!
I AM SO AWKS! SORRRRY! I'M THE CLUMSIEST EVER! I CAN'T EVEN!
OMG! SHE CAN'T EVEN! I'M WEAK!

YOU SAW THAT?
WHERE WERE YOU?
"I'M THE CLUMSIEST EVERRRR!"
GASP

I BUILT THE CHARACTER OF CLAIRE AROUND HER ID: SHE LIKES ACCESSORIES, "PRETTY" THINGS; AND WHAT GRACE MIGHT FIND APPEALING. MOST KIDS BEFRIEND PEOPLE WITH SIMILAR INTERESTS AND TASTES. THEN I CHOSE COLORS, PATTERNS, SPEECH AFFECTATION . . . THE PERFECT CANDIDATE FOR GRACE'S NEXT "BEST" FRIEND. THE REST WAS EASY!
A FEW CHANGES TO THE HAIR CAN DRAMATICALLY CHANGE THE PERCEPTION OF FACE-SHAPE.
HEADBAND: MY SISTER'S.
CLIP-ON EARRINGS: FIFTY CENTS AT A GARAGE SALE.
SHIRT: ACTUALLY, THIS IS YOURS, JAMILA. I BORROWED IT FROM YOUR DRESS-UP BOX. YOU'LL HAVE IT BACK WITHIN A WEEK.
KEEP IT.
NECKLACE: A GIFT FROM AN AUNT IN ENGLAND WHO HAS NEVER MET ME. THIS WAS ITS FIRST USE. MY MOTHER WROTE A LETTER TO MY AUNT, SHE WAS SO OVERJOYED.
SHOES, JEANS, HOODIE: ALL PICKED UP AT LOST-AND-FOUNDS. MY DRESSER IS FULL OF USEFUL ITEMS LIKE THESE, READY TO BE CALLED UPON AS NEEDED.
HOW DID YOU SEE WITHOUT YOUR GLASSES?
OH, THESE AREN'T PRESCRIPTION.
WHAT?
I JUST LIKE HOW THEY LOOK.
THEY MAKE ME LOOK SMARTER.

YOU SHOULD BE IN PLAYS. ON TV. IN MOVIES.
HAVE YOUR OWN CHANNEL.
NO THANK YOU, BUT I'LL TAKE THAT AS A COMPLIMENT.

DISGUISE IS IMPORTANT TO DETECTIVE WORK.

I'VE HAD MY EYE ON GRACE EVER SINCE I BECAME AWARE OF CHUCK AND HIS VILE BEHAVIORS.

IT WAS IN YOUR BACKYARD THAT I FIGURED OUT HOW SHE WOULD BE OF USE.
OF USE?

THIS GIRL CYCLES THROUGH BEST FRIENDS EVERY WEEK.

IF THINGS GO MY WAY, "CLAIRE" WILL QUIT AFTER-SCHOOL BAND BY NEXT FRIDAY AND GRACE'LL HAVE A NEW BEST FRIEND BY MONDAY. YOU'LL SEE.

WILL YOUR MOM LET YOU SLEEP OVER AT MY PLACE THIS WEEKEND?
SINCE THE SUMMER, MY MOM AND I HAVE GOTTEN A LOT CLOSER.

SHE PLAYS HORSE WITH ME IN THE DRIVEWAY SOMETIMES

RY
7
AND SHE'S SHOWING ME AND FAROOQ HOW TO MAKE NIHARI, OUR FAVORITE STEW.

STRANGERS AND DRIVERS AND CYCLIST
LISTS AND HOVERBOARDS AND
WHEELIE SHOES
EGWAYS AND ROLL
AND TRA
SHE'S STILL PARANOID ABOUT ME BEING OUT IN THE CITY.

BUT SHE SEEMS TO TRUST ME WITH SHIRLEY.

I'VE CAUGHT HER AND MRS. BONES ON THE PHONE TALKING ABOUT US . . .

BUT HEY, WHATEVER MAKES THEM FEEL BETTER.
GROWN-UPS ARE OBSESSED WITH THEIR KIDS SOMETIMES.

HEY!
SNAP
SNAP
SNAP

SORRY! WHAT?
CAN YOU SLEEP OVER THIS WEEKEND?

PROBABLY. I'LL ASK.
GREAT. BRING DARK CLOTHES.

MORE DRESS-UP?
YES.

Chapter 4
ANOTHER DAY, ANOTHER PRACTICE.
HEY?

YEAH?
SO HOW COME YOU'RE FRIENDS WITH THAT *SHIRLEY*?

HOW COME?
YEAH. LIKE, HOW *COME*?

I DIDN'T KNOW HOW TO ANSWER THAT.
UM. SHE'S MY FRIEND.

WE MET AT A GARAGE SALE IN THE SUMMER AND OUR MOMS LET US GO OUT ALONE IF WE PLAYED TOGETHER . . .
OOOoOOOooHHHHHHH
OKAY, I GET IT.

I DIDN'T THINK SHE DID. GET IT.

WHY?

SHE JUST SEEMS . . . NOT LIKE YOU. BUT IF YOUR MOMS MADE YOU HANG OUT, I GET IT. MY AUNTY HAS A KID THAT MY MOM MAKES ME HANG WITH WHEN SHE'S OVER.
WE'RE NOT FRIENDS, BUT SHE'S *FINE*.
THAT'S NOT REALLY—

SHIRLEY'S SUPER SERIOUS.
LIKE A LITTLE ADULT.
IT'S WEIRD.
SHE'S NOT WEIRD—

COME ON.

OKAY, SHE'S UNUSUAL, BUT—

NO, I GET IT: YOU'RE BEING NICE.
I GET IT.

UH . . .
I DIDN'T KNOW HOW TO EXPLAIN IT TO HER.

SHIRLEY'S AND MY FRIENDSHIP WAS WEIRD.
WOULD SEENA THINK IT'S TOO WEIRD?
COULDN'T I BE FRIENDS WITH BOTH OF THEM? I DIDN'T WANT TO CHOOSE...
JAMILA! SEENA! YOU'RE UP!
GOOD THING YOU MET ME—NOW YOU DON'T HAVE TO PLAY WITH SHIRLEY ALL THE TIME!
WAHEED, LET'S GO!
I DON'T—
AFTER PRACTICE, SEENA AND I PLAYED GAMES AT HER PLACE UNTIL I HAD TO BE HOME FOR DINNER. I DIDN'T KNOW HOW TO BRING IT UP AGAIN.

Chapter 5

SHIRLEY'S ROOM.
THE SLEEPOVER.

GIRLS . . .

CLICK

"YES MOTHER, WE'RE QUITE CONTENT!"

HEY MAH, WE'RE SUPES CHILL!

PFT! YOU THINK THAT'S HOW I TALK?

HA HA, NO. I'M LEARNING MUCH MORE THAN I BARGAINED FOR IN AFTER-SCHOOL BAND.
NOT ABOUT VIOLIN?

HA!

UNFORTUNATELY, THERE IS NOTHING FOR ME TO LEARN *MUSICALLY* IN AFTER-SCHOOL BAND.

BUT THE STUDY OF CHILDREN IS FASCINATING.

YOU ACT LIKE YOU AREN'T IN CLASS WITH OTHER KIDS ALL DAY!

ALSO, **YOU** ARE A KID.
YOU KNOW THAT, RIGHT?

ALL TOO WELL.

I'VE GOT ALL I CAN FROM THE KIDS IN OUR CLASS FOR NOW.

BAND IS A NEW DYNAMIC! IT MIXES KIDS FROM DIFFERENT SCHOOLS I CAN STUDY FROM **THE INSIDE**.

ARE YOU DISSECTING THEM?

AS SHIRLEY BONES, I'M ON THE OUTSIDE OBSERVING WHAT I CAN FROM CLASSMATES WHO, BY NOW, KNOW THEY ARE BEING OBSERVED.

AS CLAIRE RIVERS, IT'S ENTIRELY DIFFERENT! I'M GAINING INSIDER KNOWLEDGE!
IT'S RIVETING.

NOW YOU HAVE ALL THE COOL SLANG.
NOT **ALL**, BUT MY VOCABULARY HAS IMPROVED.
"IMPROVED"? YOU TALK BETTER THAN MOST OF OUR TEACHERS. YOU'RE ONLY GONNA GET WORSE.
BETTER AND WORSE ARE SUBJECTIVE. ALL ITERATIONS OF ENGLISH ARE VALID, AND SLANG CARRIES COMPLEX MEANINGS THAT CHARACTERIZE AND BOND GROUPS AND OFFER UNIQUE OPPORTUNITIES FOR EXPRESSION.
WHAT?
SLANG HAS VALUE EVEN THOUGH TEACHERS WILL NOT ACCEPT IT ON ASSIGNMENTS.
OH. OKAY.

HEY, SHIRLEY?
YES?

ARE YOU GETTING MORE DRESS-UP STUFF?

WHY, YES! YOU BROUGHT DARK CLOTHES?
YUP!

HA HA HA! AS IF! HA HA HAA—

UH-OH.

YOU'RE SERIOUS.
YOU CAN'T DO THAT!
YOUR MOM WILL CATCH YOU!
DIDN'T YOU HEAR? MY MOTHER IS IN HER STUDY, WATCHING *PLANET EARTH*... WHERE SHE'LL FALL ASLEEP, JUST LIKE EVERY FRIDAY.
NOTICE HOW SHE SAID "BE IN BED BY TEN"?
SHE'S A HEAVY SLEEPER. SHE'LL BE IN HER RECLINER 'TIL MORNING, LEAVING US TO TUCK OURSELVES IN. JUST LIKE EVERY FRIDAY.
NO, MY MOTHER IS NOT A CONCERN.

IF YOU COULD GET OUT OF THE HOUSE, WHERE DO THE MILTONS EVEN LIVE?
FUN FACT: RIGHT AROUND THE CORNER.

I'VE BEEN TO THEIR HOUSE, REMEMBER?
JUST ON THE OTHER SIDE OF THE PARK! A TEN MINUTE WALK... OR LESS.
I FOUND TWO GREAT SHORTCUTS.

SHIRLEY!

WAHEED, DON'T WORRY! I'VE THOUGHT THROUGH EVERY DETAIL.

I KNOW THE LAYOUT OF THEIR ENTIRE PROPERTY!

AND THE WHEREABOUTS OF EVERY MEMBER OF THE FAMILY THROUGHOUT THE NIGHT.

GRACE LIKES TO TALK.

AND I HAVE NO OTHER CHOICE.

I WOULDN'T SUGGEST THIS IF THERE WERE ANY OTHER WAY.

BESIDES, I'M A TEN-YEAR-OLD!

IF I'M CAUGHT, I'LL CHALK IT UP TO A CHILDISH PRANK! THE POLICE WILL LAUGH!
THE POLICE DON'T *ALWAYS* LAUGH.

. . . AND YOU HAVE TO ADMIT IT'S MORALLY JUSTIFIED.

BY SNEAKING IN TO TAKE BACK THE NOTE—
THE NOTE HE GOT THROUGH SHADY MEANS IN THE FIRST PLACE—
THIS ISN'T ANY WORSE THAN TAKING HIS BACKPACK AND PHONE—WHICH WE ALREADY DID!

AND YOU HELPED WITHOUT QUESTION!

IT'S NOT AS WRONG AS IT COULD BE—
IF WE *ONLY* TAKE THINGS THAT CHUCK IS USING TO BLACKMAIL EVA. AND OTHER PEOPLE.

THERE YOU HAVE IT.
ONCE YOU DECIDE IT IS DEFENSIBLE, AS I HAVE . . .
ONE MUST THEN CONSIDER RISK.

IN MY ESTIMATION, IT'S A VERY WORTHWHILE RISK.

CHUCK IS TARGETING THE MOST VULNERABLE . . .

SINCE I AM NOT VULNERABLE, AND IN A POSITION TO HELP, IS IT NOT MY RESPONSIBILITY TO DO SO?
SHE WASN'T WRONG. BUT WAS THIS JUST A PLOY TO JUSTIFY SNEAKING OUT? COULD IT BE BOTH?

HUH. BUT IT'S NOT LEGAL.

THEN AGAIN, A LOT OF REALLY BAD THINGS HAVE BEEN TECHNICALLY LEGAL.
YOU'VE SAID IT, PRECISELY!
WHILE I DON'T FLOUT THE LAW—
WHAT DOES "FLOUT" MEAN?
DISREGARD.
MOCK.
SPURN.
SCORN.
DEFY!
REPUDIATE!
IGNORE WITH DISDAIN . . .
EVEN BRAVADO!
I GET IT! I GET IT!

AS I WAS SAYING—
I SOLVE CRIMES— I HAVE TO HAVE SOME RESPECT FOR THE LAW INSOFAR AS IT BENEFITS THE MOST PEOPLE—
THAT IS SIMPLY LOGICAL.

BUT I WON'T ACCEPT LAWS THAT WERE WRITTEN TO PROTECT VERY FEW AT THE EXPENSE OF OTHERS.

LAWS WERE WRITTEN BY PEOPLE, AND CAN BE AS FLAWED AS THOSE THAT WROTE THEM.

SURE. BUT I THINK NOT BREAKING AND ENTERING PROBABLY IS A GOOD LAW.

HA!

YOU HAVE ME THERE.
BUT THERE'S NO OTHER WAY TO GET THE NOTE BACK FROM CHUCK.
HE'S HOOKED ON INTIMIDATION AND POWER.
HE'LL EXPOSE ANYONE'S SECRETS . . .
click
!

...FOR NO REASON BUT HIS OWN GAIN.
CHIPS
EITHER I DO THIS,
OR I DON'T HELP EVA AND NEXT WEEK, HER SECRET COMES OUT.
IT'LL BE SOMEONE ELSE'S SECRET THE WEEK AFTER THAT, AND THE WEEK AFTER THAT, FOREVER. IT'S TIME FOR THIS TO STOP.

AND WHILE IT MIGHT NOT FLATTER ME, I WOULD LIKE TO HAVE A WIN ON CHUCK.
HE GOT ME THE OTHER DAY—I ADMIT IT—
BUT I WILL DEFEND MY REPUTATION!
AND REMIND HIM HOW I EARNED IT.

OKAY, FINE.
WHEN DO WE LEAVE?

OH, YOU AREN'T COMING.

YOU CONVINCED ME: IT'S FAR TOO RISKY FOR **YOU** TO BE INVOLVED.
WHAT?!
FINE. THE MOMENT YOU LEAVE, I'M WAKING UP YOUR MOM AND TELLING ON YOU.
YOU CAN'T HELP ME!
HOW DO YOU KNOW? I'VE HELPED BEFORE IN WAYS YOU DIDN'T EXPECT.
FOR ALL YOU KNOW, I'M JUST THE PERSON YOU NEED TO MAKE THIS WORK.

BESIDES, IF YOUR MOM WAKES UP, HOW'S IT GOING TO LOOK IF I'M JUST HANGING OUT WHILE YOU RAN OFF?!
YOU DON'T THINK I'LL GET IN TROUBLE FOR THAT ANYWAY?
YOU'VE *MET* MY **MOTHER**.
I'M GOING, SO GET OVER IT.

SHRUG

ALL RIGHT THEN.
HEY, MAYBE WE'LL BE GROUNDED TOGETHER!

Chapter 6

DARK CLOTHES, SYNCED-UP WATCHES (SHIRLEY INSISTED PHONE SCREENS WERE TOO BRIGHT)... WE WERE READY... ALMOST.

IT WAS FUN.

UNTIL SUDDENLY...

...IT WAS TIME TO GET SERIOUS.

?
!
RIIIIIIIIIP
WHAT ARE YOU . . .

DESIST. WE ARE NOT LEAVING THAT—

I LEAVE THIS BEHIND OR WE DON'T GO AT ALL.

HMPH

We snuck out and are going to be back before 11 PM.
We're safe and no one kidnapped us. JW + SB

ZZZZZzz

BABY JACKALS ARE CALLED PUPS AND BEGIN HUNTING AS EARLY AS...

CREEEEEEEEK

GROAN

KA-CHUNK
SHUMP

GETTING OUT OF THE HOUSE: ACHIEVED.
CLICK

!

BUT WHAT IF WE COULDN'T GET BACK IN?!

MIME TRANSLATION: WHERE'S THE BACK DOOR KEY???

HA
HA
HA
HA
HA

WHEW!

HERE.
PUT THIS ON.

IF WE ARE SPOTTED WALKING AROUND IN MASKS AND SNEAK-WEAR, PEOPLE WILL KNOW WE'RE UP TO SOMETHING.

Chapter 7

IT FELT STRANGE TO BE OUT, JUST THE TWO OF US, AT NIGHT.

I NEVER DID THIS KIND OF THING BEFORE I MET SHIRLEY.

BREAKING RULES. SNEAKING AROUND.

MAYBE SHE ISN'T A NATURAL FRIEND FOR ME.
LIKE SEENA SAID.

SEENA.

I FELT GUILTY.

I STILL HADN'T TOLD HER THAT ME AND SHIRLEY WEREN'T **FORCED** TO PLAY TOGETHER.
I HAD PLENTY OF CHANCES, EVEN THAT SAME DAY.

AT SEENA'S HOUSE, AFTER PRACTICE.
ONLY TWENTY MORE MINUTES, THEN YOU DO SOMETHING WITH NO SCREENS.
OKAY ABU!
DUNK! HAHAHA!
NICE!

I'D HATE TO BE FRIENDS WITH SOMEONE WHO ISN'T INTO BASKETBALL.

CLICK
CLICK
CLICK
CLICK
CLICK
MY SISTER'S BEST FRIEND DOESN'T CARE ABOUT MOVIES, AND THAT'S THE **ONLY** THING MY SISTER LIKES.
CLICK
CLICK
CLICK
CLICK
CLICK

WHAT DO THEY EVEN TALK ABOUT?!
THAT WOULD HAVE BEEN A GREAT TIME TO SAY SOMETHING.
HEH.
YEAH.
(NOT THAT.)

I HAD A MOMENT . . .

HA!
GOT THE BALL!

!

. . .

MASH

KEEP UP, WAHEED!

WHAT?!

YOU BUTTHEAD!
I'M COMING
FOR IT!

. . . BUT I DIDN'T
TAKE IT.

SEENA LIKES ALL THE SAME STUFF I DO.
SHE GETS THE SAME JOKES AND REFERENCES.
SHE DOESN'T THINK MY FAMILY IS WEIRD.
I LIKE BEING HER FRIEND.
I'VE GOTTEN INTO TROUBLE WITH SHIRLEY BEFORE . . .
IF WE GET CAUGHT, WE'LL BE IN BIG TROUBLE *RIGHT NOW.*

IS SHE ACTUALLY A GOOD FRIEND FOR ME?
AHH!!
CAN I TELL YOU A SECRET?
I HAVE ALWAYS SECRETLY THOUGHT
THAT IF I HAD A MIND TO SNEAK AROUND, OR LIE OR GET INTO CRIME OF ANY SORT . . .
I'D BE QUITE GOOD AT IT.
I'VE THOUGHT SO TOO.
YOU HAVE?

WELL. THIS IS MY
CHANCE TO TEST
IT OUT, I SUPPOSE.

THIS IS A BLUE LIGHT.

MUCH LESS BRIGHT THAN THE USUAL WHITE OR YELLOW.

A NOTEBOOK,
A MAGNIFYING GLASS,
TALCUM POWDER
OOH!
A PAIR OF THIN GLOVES,
SCOTCH TAPE,
A FLASHLIGHT,
BABY POWDER,
LOCK-PICKING KIT
I'M SAVING UP FOR A POCKET RECORDER THAT COULD BE PLANTED IN A SECRET LOCATION THAT TRANSMITS SOUND FILES REMOTELY.
ZZZ!!!!IP

GRACE IS DEVOTED TO SOME INANE TELEVISION PROGRAM THAT SHE WATCHES WITHOUT FAIL IN HER BEDROOM EVERY FRIDAY FROM NINE TO TEN PM.

CHUCK IS GAMING IN THE BASEMENT FROM NINE THIRTY PM ONWARD—HE PLAYS ONLINE WITH FRIENDS, SO THEY'RE STRICT ABOUT THE TIME, AND ARE NEVER TO BE INTERRUPTED.

GRACE SAYS HE PILES SNACKS ON THE COFFEE TABLE AND PLAYS FOR HOURS AT A TIME, ONLY TAKING BREAKS TO USE THE WASHROOM—ALSO IN THE BASEMENT—SO WE'RE NOT GOING TO RUN INTO HIM.

THEIR PARENTS ARE WILD CARDS.
BY REMARKABLE COINCIDENCE, THEY RECEIVED SOME UNEXPECTED MAIL THAT WILL TAKE THEM OUT OF THE HOUSE THIS VERY NIGHT.
Mr. & Mrs. Milton
Toronto, ON
DINNER THEATRE
ANOTHER CLIENT WORKS FOR HER PARENTS' THEATER COMPANY AND WAS SUPPOSED TO HELP DRUM UP A NEW AUDIENCE.
VIP
VIP
SUDDENLY THE MILTONS GET TICKETS IN THE MAIL; TWO BIRDS WITH ONE STONE.

SUCCESSFUL DETECTIVE WORK IS OFTEN COLLECTING SMALL DOTS OF INFORMATION AND THEN FINDING THE MOST LOGICAL WAY TO CONNECT THE DOTS. USING WHAT'S AVAILABLE.
ONE NEVER KNOWS WHAT INFORMATION MIGHT BE USEFUL.
OH, WE'RE GETTING CLOSER. THAT'S THEIR HOUSE . . .
. . . THERE.
GULP.

WHOA.
IT'S FANCY.
OH YES, THE MILTONS
ARE VERY WELL-OFF.

YET ANOTHER
REASON CHUCK IS
DEPLORABLE—

HE'S NOT DOING THIS BECAUSE HE
NEEDS THE MONEY. HE JUST LIKES
HAVING POWER OVER PEOPLE.

LET'S SUIT
UP AGAIN.

AM I REALLY DOING THIS?

CRACK
CRACK
CRUNCH
SNAP
WE GOT QUIET AGAIN.
CRUNCH

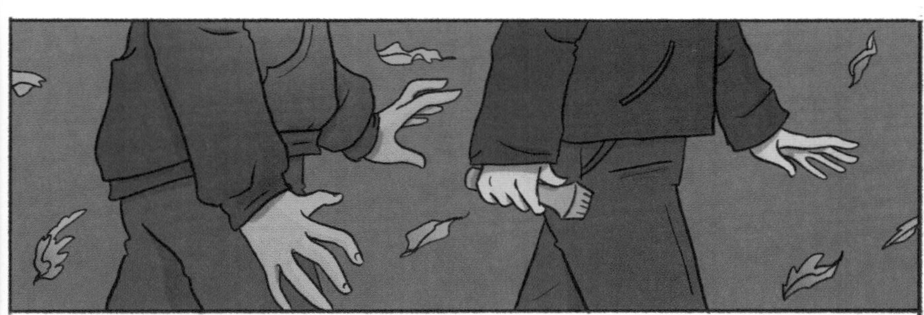

SUDDENLY IT FELT **REAL**.

Chapter 8
WE WERE REALLY DOING THIS.

BEWARE OF DOG

BEWARE OF DOG

SHIRLEY'S WHISPER WAS ALMOST SILENT. LIKE THE VOICE OF A MOTH.
THE SIGN IS A FAKE.

THEY WANT TO SCARE PEOPLE OFF BUT DON'T WANT TO HAVE TO TAKE CARE OF A REAL DOG.

CLICK
CLACK

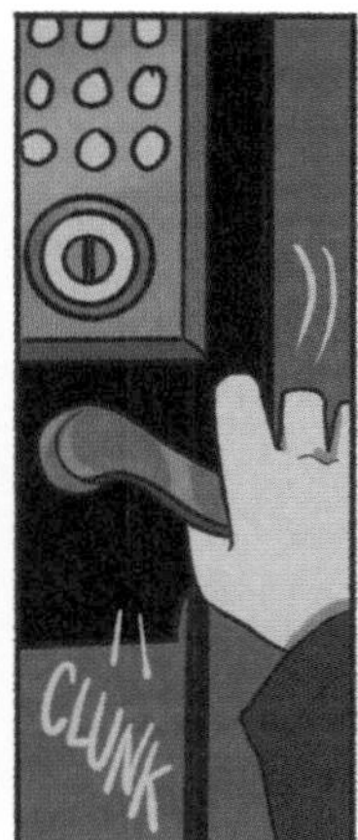
CLUNK

I BET YOUR "BEST FRIEND" GRACE GAVE YOU THE CODE?

SHE DID A VERY BAD JOB OF HIDING IT.

THERE WE WERE.
INSIDE THE MILTONS' YARD.

SHIRLEY EXPLAINED:
THAT'S GRACE, WATCHING HER SHOW IN HER ROOM.
CHUCK, PLAYING VIDEO GAMES IN THE BASEMENT.
CHUCK'S BEDROOM. WHERE WE ARE GOING.
HE HAS HIS OWN BALCONY?
YEESH.

THAT'S OUR ENTRY POINT.
THE BACK DOOR LEADS INTO THE KITCHEN, WHERE THERE'S A REAR STAIRWAY.
WE CAN TAKE THAT UP TO CHUCK'S ROOM (KEEP OUT STICKERS).
KEEP OUT!
GET LOST!
WITHOUT PASSING GRACE'S DOOR (HEART STICKERS).
ONCE WE'RE IN, WE FIND THE SAFE. I'LL TAKE IT FROM THERE.

SHIRLEY SEEMED SO CONFIDENT.
I COULDN'T HELP FEELING LIKE WE WEREN'T ALONE.

SHIRLEY?
YES?

IT'S ALREADY 9:40 PM.
THIS IS DIFFERENT THAN MY BACK DOOR . . .

TAP
TAP
PLEASE DON'T BUMP ME WHILE I'M DOING THIS.

SNATCH

!

I DIDN'T EVEN TRY THE DOOR FIRST.
WHAT?

LOOK.
IT WAS **ALREADY** UNLOCKED.

WHY LEAVE IT OPEN? I DON'T LIKE IT.

BUT WE HAVE TO
HURRY.

WE'LL KEEP IT UNLOCKED.
RATTLE

Chapter 9

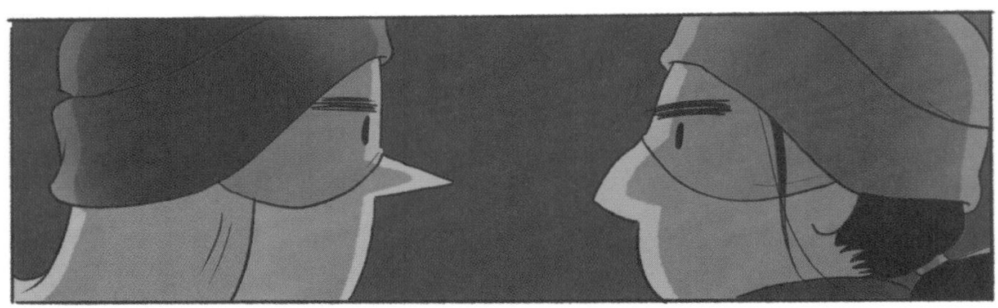

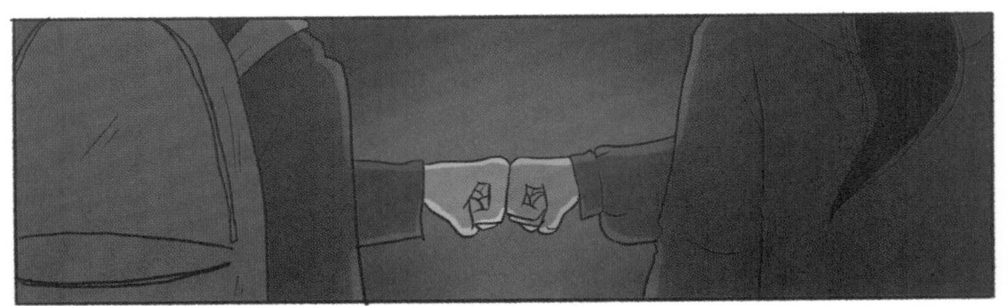

THAT'S THE STAIRS TO THE BASEMENT...

WHERE CHUCK...

IS PLAYING VIDEO GAMES.

SHIRLEY ONLY USED HAND GESTURES, BUT I KNEW EXACTLY WHAT SHE MEANT.

KA-
CHUNK

AS I CLIMBED UP THE MILTONS' STAIRS,
WITH EACH STEP, I FELT NEW FEELINGS RISING UP ALONG WITH ME.
I FELT AWARE, AND ALERT IN A NEW WAY.
I WAS SCARED
BUT EXCITED TOO.
I FELT. . . ALIVE.
AT THAT MOMENT, THERE WAS NOWHERE ELSE I'D RATHER BE THAN IN A CREEPY STAIRWELL, SERIOUSLY BREAKING RULES—BUT TO HELP SOMEONE—WITH SHIRLEY.

TOP
CAUTION CAUTION CAUT
KEEP OUT
AUTION CAUTION CAUT

TOP
CAUTION CAUTION CAU
KEEP OUT
ON CAUTION CAU

HERE'S THE PLAN: I'VE GOT THE NUMBERS TO THE SAFE'S PUNCH CODE,

BUT I DON'T KNOW THEIR ORDER. I'VE TIMED IT: I NEED SEVEN MINUTES TO TRY ALL THE VARIATIONS.

YOU STAND BY THE DOOR AND IF YOU HEAR ANYONE COMING, LOCK IT, AND WE'LL ESCAPE THROUGH THE EN SUITE BATHROOM.

"ON SWEET" BATHROOM?

beep boop

THAT BATHROOM! IT HAS TWO DOORS— YOU GET INTO IT FROM CHUCK'S ROOM, AND LEAVE INTO THE HALLWAY!

Mick & Shorty
19
POW

THAT'S JUST WHAT WE DID.

SEVEN MINUTES IS A LONG TIME TO STAND QUIETLY IN THE DARK. TRY IT. YOU'LL SEE.

I'VE GONE TO HER HOUSE A FEW TIMES TOO.

YES, I KNOW.

YOU DO?
BY THEN, I SHOULDN'T HAVE BEEN SURPRISED.

OKAY. WELL, SHE WAS ASKING ABOUT YOU.

AND SHE GOT IT IN HER MIND THAT WE WERE . . .
YES?

THAT WE WERE JUST FRIENDS BECAUSE OUR PARENTS **MAKE** US.

AND BEFORE I COULD SAY ANYTHING, THE COACH CALLED US AND I DIDN'T TELL HER DIFFERENT AND . . .

I JUST WANTED TO SAY . . .

I DON'T THINK THAT.

I LIKE BEING
FRIENDS WITH YOU.

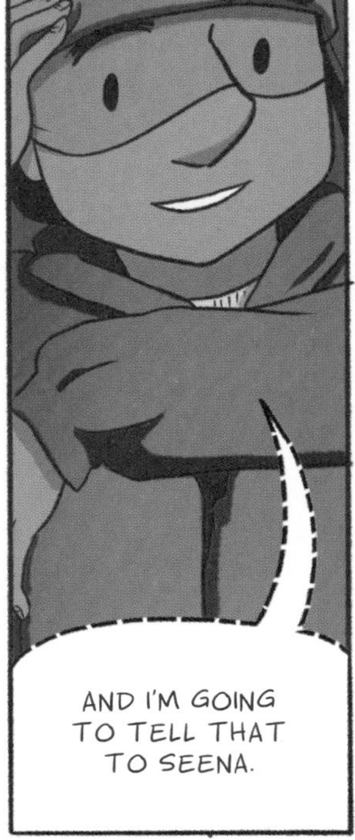

YOU'D LIKE SEENA.
WE SHOULD—
YES!
I HAVEN'T
EVEN—
IT'S OPEN.

WHOA.

I CAN'T READ IN THE DARK. WHICH ONE IS EVA'S?
IT DOESN'T MATTER.

WE'RE TAKING ALL OF THEM.

!
. . .

MAYBE YOU, ME, AND SEENA CAN—
SHH!

HEY, I'M JUST—

GASP

CLAMP

THERE WAS STILL STUFF IN THE SAFE, BUT I DIDN'T DARE SAY ANYTHING.
SHIRLEY'S GLARE HAD MADE THAT CLEAR.
SHOVE

IT WAS SO QUIET, I THOUGHT SHIRLEY HAD BEEN HEARING THINGS. I WAS GOING TO ASK HER—
BUT SHE SQUEEZED MY HAND SO TIGHTLY,
I KNEW TO KEEP QUIET.

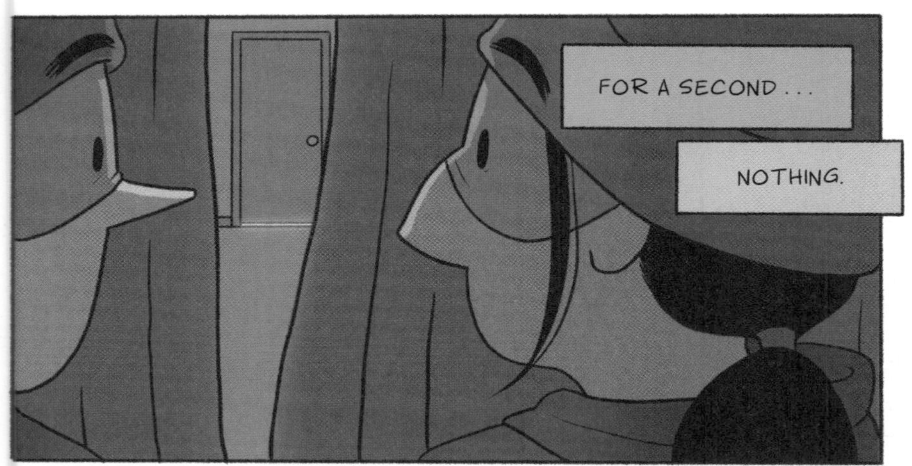
FOR A SECOND . . .
NOTHING.

THEN . . .
RATTLE

CHUCK HIMSELF!

CREEEEEEEAAAAAAK
KSSSSTTT

SLUUURRRRRRRRRP

CLUNK
KRINKLE
KRINKLE
CRUNCH
CRUNCH

MINUTES PASSED. I DON'T KNOW HOW MANY.
A PART OF ME WANTED TO STEP OUT AND CONFESS,
BUT SHIRLEY GAVE ME A LITTLE HAND SQUEEZE OF CONFIDENCE, AND A LOOK THAT SOMEHOW REASSURED ME: SHE'S GOT THIS.
I FELT CONFIDENCE AND EXCITEMENT FLOOD BACK INTO ME.
WE GOT THIS.

WHAT WOULD WE DO IF CHUCK SAW THE SAFE?
KNOWING SHIRLEY, SHE ALREADY HAD A PLAN, BUT SINCE SHE COULDN'T TELL ME, I NEEDED MY OWN.
SSSSLLUUURRRRP
BURP
WHILE CHUCK CHEWED AND SMACKED AND SLURPED (SO GROSS), I PLANNED:
PLAN A:
chuck sees open safe.
I PUNCH CHUCK.
I Get creamed.
BAD PLAN.

PLAN B:

Chuck sees Safe. I jump out... & distract him with a DANCE?

TERRIBLE PLAN.

LOOK AROUND.

USE WHAT'S AVAILABLE.

PLAN C:

Chuck sees Safe.

Use Blanket!

Hold as long as I can. Leave the Rest to Shirley.

GOOD PLAN.

SSLUR
I FIGURED ONCE HE FINISHED THE SODA, MAYBE THEN HE'D LEAVE.

AHH

CLUNK

TO PASS THE TIME I TRIED TO FIGURE HOW MANY MORE SIPS 'TIL IT WAS DONE . . .

BOOP

BLOO

BLUP

BOO

PEW

PEW

PEW

BEEP

I GUESSED NINE.

SLUUURRRP

BOOP
BOOP
BOOP
BLEEP
SLUUURRRPPP
PEW
PEW
PEW
PEW
PEW
SLUUURRRR
I HAD COUNTED TO THREE . . .
WHEN SHIRLEY GAVE ME A **LOOK**. BUT WHY?
HER HEARING IS SURE SOMETHING BECAUSE I LISTENED **HARD** AND HEARD **NOTHING** . . .
TAP
TAP
UNTIL SUDDENLY, TAPPING! AT CHUCKS DOOR!

SLUUUUUUUU
UUUURRRRF
-RRRPPPP
CLICK
AHH
IT WASN'T GRACE.
OR THE PARENTS HOME EARLY.
IT WAS SOMEONE NEW.

Chapter 10

YOU'RE LATE.
I TRUST YOU FOUND THE DOOR UNLOCKED.
HE WAS EXPECTING SOMEONE!

SLUUURRRPPPP!

I MISSED A NIGHT OF GAMING FOR THIS, SO IT BETTER BE WORTH IT.

LET'S SEE . . .
SWIPE
YOU HAVE LETTERS FROM YOUR FRIEND.
OR SHOULD I SAY *EX-FRIEND?*
SNORT
AND YOU THINK THEY MAY BE OF INTEREST TO ME.

WELL, I'LL NEED TO SEE THE LETTERS—
ORIGINALS, NOT COPIES—
AND IF THEY LIVE UP TO THE HYPE
WE JUST NEED TO FIND A PRICE—
WHOA! IT'S YOU!

IT'S **WHO**?! I WANTED TO GET A BETTER LOOK,
BUT COULDN'T RISK ANY MOVEMENT THAT MIGHT GIVE US AWAY.

YEAH, YOU KNOW ME PRETTY WELL, I THINK.

YOU MIGHT REMEMBER ME FROM HAVING **RUINED MY LIFE**.

PROBABLY RINGS A BELL.

HEH HEH HEH
FEEL
GLUG
CLUNK
LISTEN FRIEND,
YOU WERE SO STUBBORN!
WHY DID YOU MAKE ME DO SOMETHING SO,
LIKE, EXTREME?
I DON'T HURT PEOPLE—
I HELP THEM.
BUT I HAVE TO GET MINE. IT'S ONLY FAIR.

I TOLD YOU MY PRICE AND YOU DECIDED TO CALL MY BLUFF,
PAL-STER.
NOT MUCH CHOICE LEFT FOR OL' CHUCKIE BOY,
YOU FEEL ME?
SNORT
IT'S NOT ENOUGH FOR YOU TO BE A TERRIBLE, TOTALLY WRETCHED HUMAN...

. . . BUT YOU SPREAD YOUR SICKO VIBES TO ALL THE OTHER KIDS!

RUSTLE

CRINKLE

CRINKL

RUSTLE

AND NOW EVERY PLACE IS CRAWLING WITH YOUR SCUMMY LITTLE MINIONS.

BOOT-LICKERS, CREEPING ON EVERYONE, JUST LOOKING FOR A FREE JELLYBEAN FROM YOU . . .

CRUNCH

CRONCH

IN EXCHANGE FOR PICTURES AND LETTERS AND **VIDEOS** . . .

LIKE THE ONE YOUR BRAT-
BRIGADE GOT OF ME!
IT WAS **SEENA**!

THE ONE TIME I EVER SLIPPED UP!
WHAT HAD SHE DONE?
I MADE AMENDS, YOU KNOW. I MADE IT RIGHT ON MY END,
WITH MY FAMILY, WITH MY CONSCIENCE . . .
BUT THAT'S NOT ENOUGH FOR YOU.
YOU SPUN IT LIKE I WAS A MONSTER.
YOU SPREAD THE WORD UNTIL YOU HAD PARENTS CALLING MY HOUSE, CALLING MY TEACHERS!
TEACHERS WHO SUPPORTED AND BELIEVED IN ME!

I HAD BEGGED YOU NOT TO SEND IT OUT

ER
AND YOU LAUGHED IN MY FACE,

HEH HUR
LIKE YOU'RE TRYING TO LAUGH NOW

BUT I CAN SEE YOU SHAKING, YOU EEL.

NOT SO FUNNY WHEN I'M IN YOUR HOUSE,

WHEN I DON'T HAVE ANYTHING ELSE TO LOSE.

IS IT?

IS IT FUNNY?

CHUCK?
JAB

YOU CAN'T PUSH
ME AROUND IN MY HOUSE!
I'LL SHOUT AND MY PARENTS
WILL COME FLYING IN AND
HAVE YOU PUT BEHIND BARS
WHERE YOU BELONG!

I TRIED TO MOVE ON, BUT THERE ARE GOOD KIDS AT YOUR SCHOOL. KIDS THAT YOU COULD STILL MESS WITH, AND I'M NOT LETTING THAT HAPPEN.
YOU AREN'T GOING TO HURT ANYONE ANYMORE, CHUCK.

WHAT YOU DO, WHY YOU DO IT:
IT'S **GROSS**. AND IT'S OVER.

TIME FOR A NEW HOBBY,
LITTLE BUDDY.

SHE WAS PLAYING FOR TIME.
CROSS-STITCH IS POPULAR. YOU SHOULD TRY IT. KEEP THOSE HANDS AND THOSE BEADY LITTLE EYES *BUSY.*
CHUCK WAS FIGURING IT OUT TOO.

HEH
HEH
HEH
UH-OH.

BIG WORDS,
BIG WORDS.

ANYTHING ELSE YOU WANT TO MONOLOGUE ABOUT WHILE YOU LOOK AROUND FOR SOMETHING TO PIN ON ME?

I'LL TAKE "STALLING" FOR 1000, ALEX!

THERE'S A REAL FUN TREND OF KIDS THINKING THEY CAN JUST GRAB MY PHONE OR STEAL MY BACKPACK LIKE THAT'S GOING TO DO ANYTHING.
I AM SMARTER THAN YOU.
SO SMART IN FACT, I'LL POINT YOU RIGHT TO WHAT YOU'RE LOOKING AROUND IN VAIN FOR: MY 180-POUND, LOCKED SAFE!
POWER

EVEN IF YOU COULD CARRY IT OUT OF HERE, WHICH YOU CAN'T,
YOU'D STILL HAVE TO CONTEND WITH THE COMBINA—
...
WHAT
HOW DID YOU-

MMMMF!!!
UNGH!
!@
MM! *
@!!!
HOW DARE YOU!?!
*
MY PARENTS!!
*
MMM!!
SEENA.
STOP.

I DON'T KNOW HOW YOU DID THIS, BUT YOU AREN'T GETTING PAST ME WITH THOSE.
BYE, CHUCK.

WAIT!
KEEP YOUR HANDS RIGHT THERE OR I'M GONE.
WHAT.

YOU CAN'T TAKE THOSE.
I'LL HAVE NOTHING.
LOOK AROUND!

YOU HAVE EVERYTHING.
19

I WANT...
I WANT WHAT YOU HAVE!
WHAT'S THAT?
YOU TOOK EVERYTHING AWAY FROM ME! MY WHOLE LIFE!
I MADE A NEW ONE THAT YOU CAN'T TOUCH ANYMORE!
WHAT DO I HAVE THAT YOU WANT?
YOU KNOW...
YOU WERE ALWAYS LAUGHING...
OTHER KIDS, TEACHERS, PARENTS...
THEY LIKE YOU.

YOU WON'T GET THAT WITH THESE.

I'M ACTUALLY DOING YOU A FAVOR.
TRY MAKING SOME ACTUAL FRIENDS.

NOT JUST KIDS WHO WANT SOMETHING OR ARE SCARED OF YOU.

BUT I'M TAKING THESE.

YOU'RE WELCOME.

CHOMP

AHHHHHHHH
RRRRRRAAAAAAAAAA

HE'S HEADED FOR THE BACKYARD. WE'LL GO OUT THE FRONT. HURRY.

SEENA GOT AWAY BEFORE CHUCK EVEN MADE IT DOWN THE STAIRS.

SHE REALLY IS GOOD.

NO TIME
FOR CAUTION—
WE JUST RAN.

WAIT!

IF WE DON'T LOCK THE DOOR BEHIND US, THEY'LL KNOW SOMEONE ELSE WAS—
BOOP
WHHIIIIIRRR
CLUNK
LOCKED.
WE WERE NEVER HERE. NOW LET'S GO!

WE RAN ALL THE WAY TO SHIRLEY'S HOUSE WITHOUT STOPPING.
I BARELY REMEMBER IT.

IN SHIRLEY'S YARD, WE FINALLY STOPPED TO CATCH OUR BREATH. WE WEREN'T IN THE CLEAR YET.
PANT
PANT
WE ESCAPED CHUCK'S, BUT THERE WERE OTHER WAYS TO GET CAUGHT.

WE CHECKED OUR WATCHES—
THE WHOLE EPISODE BARELY TOOK AN HOUR!

MASKS OFF—LESS QUESTIONS IF SOMEONE IS UP.

A CLICK.
A STEP.
A SNORE.
ZZZZZ

CLUNK
AND WE WERE BACK.
AS IF WE'D NEVER LEFT.

WE COULDN'T WAIT TO TALK ABOUT IT, BUT AGREED TO GET OUR PAJAMAS ON FIRST AND CHAT IN THE DARK.

ZZZZZ
ZZZZ

WE BROKE INTO THE HOUSE OF A SERIAL BLACKMAILER, ONLY TO WITNESS HIM THWARTED BY HIS VICTIM, WHO STOLE ALL OF HIS TREASURES

AND FLED OUT AN OPEN SECOND-STORY BALCONY.

WELL,

THAT SOUNDS LIKE QUITE AN EVENING.

Chapter 11
WALKING TO SCHOOL ON MONDAY MORNING, NEITHER OF US WAS CHATTY . . .
BUT EVEN WITHOUT TALKING, I FELT AN EXTRA-FRIENDLY FEELING BETWEEN SHIRLEY AND ME.
NO ONE IS ILLEGAL
WE DIDN'T HAVE EVERYTHING IN COMMON, BUT WHAT WE HAD, COUNTED.

THE LUCKY THING IS YOU GET TO HAVE MORE THAN ONE FRIEND.

DID EVERYBODY KNOW THIS? IT'S FUNNY I WAS JUST FIGURING IT OUT.

I COULDN'T STOP THINKING ABOUT SEENA . . .
AFTER BREAKFAST ON SATURDAY, SHIRLEY AND I TALKED ABOUT WHAT DO TO WITH ALL OF THE EVIDENCE WE STOLE.

WE HAVE THE FOLLOWING OPTIONS: DESTROY THEM OR RETURN THEM.

BUT RETURN THEM TO WHO? A BUNCH OF PEOPLE COULD BE INVOLVED—HOW DO WE KNOW WHICH KID WAS CHUCK'S TARGET?

WHY DON'T WE WAIT AND SEE WHAT SEENA DOES? SHE GOT BURNED BY CHUCK . . .

SHE KNOWS HOW IT FEELS.

WE AGREED THAT WAS THE BEST PLAN AND TUCKED THE BACKPACK AWAY.

FOR NOW.

SHIRLEY SAID ALL WE HAD TO DO NOW WAS WAIT FOR THE REPERCUSSIONS.

THEN SHE HAD TO EXPLAIN WHAT "REPERCUSSIONS" MEANT.

"THE EFFECT OR RESULT OF AN ACTION."

BASICALLY, "WHAT HAPPENS NEXT."

THE HALLWAY WAS *BUZZING.*

WHAT'S GOING ON?

YOU KNOW CHUCK? THAT AWESOME SIXTH GRADER WHO ALWAYS HAS CANDY?

SURE. WHAT ABOUT HIM?
HE GOT BROKEN INTO! AT HIS HOUSE!

RRRRIIIIIIIINNGGGG
HOW DID YOU HEAR THIS?
EVERYBODY KNOWS!
I GOTTA GO!

WE WERE ITCHING FOR MORE INFORMATION.

AT RECESS, WE GOT IT.
I'VE TALKED TO A FEW KIDS, ALL THEY SAY IS "HIS HOUSE GOT BROKEN INTO."
NO ONE IS TALKING ABOUT THE NOTES, THE EVIDENCE— ABOUT ANYTHING THAT GOT TAKEN.

CHUCK WOULDN'T TELL PEOPLE—IT'S IN HIS BEST INTERESTS TO PRETEND HE STILL HOLDS HIS OLD POWER.

I WONDER—
SHIRLEY BONES.

SHAY PARK.
SHAY, THIS IS JAMIL—
I NEED TO TALK TO *YOU.*
JAMILA'S WITH ME. SHE STAYS.
FINE.
LISTEN. DO YOU KNOW GRACE MILTON?
I KNOW **OF** HER, BUT WE'VE NEVER MET.
WELL, MY *BEST FRIEND* GRACE'S BROTHER . . .
JUST GOT TOTALLY ROBBED IN THEIR OWN HOUSE! AND GRACE TOTALLY SAW WHO DID IT!
KIDS. TWO GIRLS ALL IN BLACK! ONE WITH A DARK PONYTAIL!

GRACE JUST SAW THEM LEAVING.

IN MASKS.

THAT'S WHAT ROBBERS WEAR.

HER BROTHER CHUCK'S DOOR WAS OPEN,
BUT WHEN SHE TOLD HIM WHAT SHE SAW, HE SAID SHE WAS JUST MAKING IT UP FOR ATTENTION!
HE TOLD HER TO SHUT UP ABOUT IT AND THAT SHE BETTER NOT TELL ANYBODY.
SHE'S TRYING TO HELP HIM!
SO THE DESCRIPTION IS TWO KIDS, ONE HAS A DARK PONYTAIL?
NOD
UH-HUH.
NOTHING ELSE?
NUH-UH.
KID IN A MASK, WITH A DARK PONYTAIL . . .
THAT COULD BE ANYONE . . .

YOU COULD BE DESCRIBING JAMILA HERE, FOR HOW COMMON THAT IS.

NO, I DON'T THINK THIS IS THE CASE FOR ME.

BESIDES, I HEAR CHUCK IS QUITE CAPABLE OF HANDLING HIS OWN AFFAIRS.

OH, HE'S A TOTAL JERK. SHE SAW THESE TWO GIRLS LEAVING OUT THE FRONT DOOR!!

BOYS NEVER BELIEVE GIRLS. IT'S SO STUPID.

INDEED, IT IS.

SORRY I CAN'T HELP.

AH, IT'S OKAY. CHUCK CAN WORK IT OUT ON HIS OWN.

Chapter 12

I TEXTED SEENA TO MEET ME HERE. WHERE IS SHE? HOW LONG'S THE WALK FROM HER SCHOOL? TEN MINUTES? FIFTEEN?
ANNEX ELEMENTARY. AFTER SCHOOL, OUTSIDE THE GYM.
YOU'RE NERVOUS.

I DON'T KNOW WHAT TO SAY! HOW DO I EXPLAIN THAT WE WERE THERE?

MAYBE YOU SHOULD STAY AND HELP ME EXPLAIN.
YES, MY FAMOUS TACT AND DELICACY WILL HELP.

HA HA HA HA HA

I THINK YOU NEED TO DO THIS ON YOUR OWN. AT LEAST AT FIRST. MAYBE I'LL JOIN YOU IN A BIT.
ARG! WE DON'T EVEN KNOW HER BIG SECRET! WHAT'S ON CHUCK'S VIDEO?

SHE'S AT A NEW SCHOOL THIS YEAR, RIGHT?
YEAH . . .
HAVE YOU EVER ASKED HER ABOUT HER OLD SCHOOL?

SHE DOESN'T SEEM TO WANT TO TALK ABOUT IT . . .
HMM.

HAVE YOU EVER PARTICIPATED IN STUDENT GOVERNMENT?
WHAT?

SHIRLEY, YOU ARE THE QUEEN OF BRINGING UP RANDOM THINGS!
NON SEQUITURS.

WHAT!?
A NON SEQUITUR IS SOMETHING THAT SEEMS TO COME OUT OF NOWHERE, CONVERSATIONALLY.

FINE. YOU ARE THE QUEEN OF "NON SEQUITURS."

THAT WASN'T A NON SEQUITUR.
VOTE
FOR MIDDLE YEARS CLASS PRESIDENT
HERE COMES SEENA.
I'LL BE BACK.
F-11

IS THIS YOU?

YEAH . . .

WAIT, IS YOUR OLD SCHOOL **MY** SCHOOL?

YUP.

I DIDN'T USED TO BE SO INTO BASKETBALL.

I USED TO BE ALL ABOUT STUDENT GOVERNMENT.

IN GRADE FOUR—TWO YEARS AGO—I RAN FOR MIDDLE YEARS PRESIDENT—THEY REPRESENT GRADES FOUR AND FIVE—
HASEENA
FOR
MIDDLE
YEARS
CLASS
PRESIDENT
AND I WON.

I'D GO WITH THE UPPER YEARS' PRESIDENT TO A MONTHLY STAFF MEETING AND TELL THE TEACHERS AND PRINCIPAL WHAT STUDENTS WANT.

USUAL STUFF YOU WON'T EVER GET LIKE LONGER RECESS AND NO TESTS . . .
TOP STUDENT REQUESTS
• NO TESTS, EVER.
• 5 RECESSES PER DAY.
• TEACHERS NICER, NEVER MEAN.
• MORE FUN CLASSES (GYM, ART, DRAMA)
PIZZA DAY EVERY DAY
NEW TO CANADA? TORONTO?? THIS SCHOOL???
JOIN US!!!
SIGN UP
BUT ALSO WE STARTED THE NEWCOMERS CLUB FOR KIDS WHO JUST MOVED TO CANADA,

WHICH HAD A SPIN-OFF: THE INTERNATIONAL LUNCH CLUB—THAT WAS REALLY POPULAR IN THE END—

WHO IS YOUR
COUNCILLOR?
MP?
MPP?
MAYOR?
PREMIER?
• BLM • MMIW
• FOOD JUSTICE
STOP CLIMATE
AND SOCIAL JUSTICE CLUB, WHERE WE WRITE REPRESENTATIVES AND TALK ABOUT OTHER WAYS KIDS CAN PROTEST.

YOU STARTED THOSE?
DO YOU KNOW MRS. LEZAMA?

THAT'S MY TEACHER! SHE'S REALLY GOOD. SHE WAS SO NICE WHEN I FIRST STARTED THIS YEAR.
YEAH, SHE'S GREAT.

ALL THOSE CLUBS NEED A TEACHER SUPERVISOR AND SHE HELPED SO MUCH
AND GOT OTHER GOOD TEACHERS INVOLVED TOO.

SHE WAS THE ONE WHO FIRST SUGGESTED I RUN, BACK WHEN I WAS IN HER CLASS.
STUDENT GOVERNMENT COULD BE A GREAT PLACE TO HONE YOUR SKILLS, SEENA.

HONE?
SHARPEN.
YOU HAVE GOOD IDEAS, A SENSE OF COMMUNITY, AND NATURAL LEADERSHIP SKILLS.
WE NEED ALL THE GOOD LEADERS WE CAN GET.

BEFORE I RAN, I SAT IN ON SOME STUDENT GOVERNMENT MEETINGS TO CHECK IT OUT, BUT THE KIDS SEEMED WAY OLDER. IT WAS REAL INTIMIDATING—
ESPECIALLY TO KIDS MY AGE.

SO ONCE I WAS ELECTED, I PUSHED FOR MORE YOUNG PEOPLE,
BY ADDING A JR. VICE PRESIDENT...

JUNIOR
VICE PRESIDENT
IT COULD BE
YOU!
SIGN UP HERE
chuck
... WHICH CHUCK WON.

AFTER GETTING ELECTED, HE GOT REALLY OUT OF HAND.
THE VICE PRESIDENT WAS SUPPOSED TO GET MORE KIDS **INVOLVED**.

CHUCK JUST WANTED MORE KIDS TO ORDER AROUND.

HE ALSO USED MEETING TIME TO TRY AND GET ME, AS PRESIDENT, TO BRING UP **HIS** INTERESTS WITH THE TEACHERS.

SOME WERE THINGS ALL THE KIDS WANTED.
MORE PHONE TIME!
PIZZA DAYS!
YOU KNOW.

BUT OTHER THINGS HE BROUGHT UP WOULD ONLY HELP HIM AND OTHER RICH KIDS. LIKE FANCY FIELD TRIPS PARENTS HAVE TO PAY **A TON** EXTRA FOR.

HE DIDN'T EVEN PUSH TO FUND-RAISE OR GET THE SCHOOL TO COVER KIDS WHO COULDN'T PAY—CHUCK JUST WANTED MORE FOR **HIM**.

I REFUSED, OBVIOUSLY.

!

BUT THEN I'D FIND OUT HE WAS TALKING TO THE TEACHERS—

TELLING THEM THAT I WASN'T LISTENING TO HIM, THAT I WASN'T "REPRESENTING STUDENT NEEDS" ON COUNCIL.

MOST OF THE TEACHERS KNEW ME WELL ENOUGH TO KNOW THIS WASN'T TRUE.

BUT SOME TEACHERS— ONES WHO DIDN'T COME TO THE MONTHLY MEETINGS THEMSELVES, OR THE FEW WHO HADN'T SUPPORTED MY CLUBS— WERE LISTENING.

I JUST DON'T HAVE BULLETIN BOARD SPACE TO SPARE FOR THESE "SPECIAL INTEREST" GROUPS—
MRS. WHITE, IT'S A *STUDENT* CLUB. ANYONE CAN JOIN—
INTERNATIONAL LUNCH CLUB
HE WAS PLANTING SEEDS.

THEN IT WAS GRADE FIVE—LAST YEAR. I WAS VOTED IN AS MIDDLE GRADE PRESIDENT AGAIN!
RE-ELECT
HASEENA

AFTER A YEAR OF EXPERIENCE, I WAS CONFIDENT, AND READY!

CHUCK WASN'T HAPPY. HE MADE VICE PRESIDENT AGAIN, BUT THAT WASN'T ENOUGH. HE WANTED THE TOP SPOT.

THE YEAR WAS GOOD AT FIRST! THE NEW UPPER YEARS' CABINET WERE COOL AND REALLY NICE TO ME.
SHE'S SO CUTE!
HANG OUT WITH US!
YOU'RE SO SMART FOR YOUR AGE!

THEY TREATED ME KINDA LIKE A PET . . .
AND I ADMIT I LIKED THE ATTENTION.

MY PARENTS WERE HAPPY—THEY LET ME SPEND WAY MORE UNSUPERVISED TIME WITH MY NEW OLDER FRIENDS,
ASSUMING WE WERE DOING GOVERNMENT STUFF.

OPEN
BUT HALF THE TIME THE GIRLS WANTED TO HANG OUT BY CORNER STORES, GETTING SLUSHIES . . .

AND AS I FOUND OUT,
STEALING STUFF.

IT SOUNDS BAD NOW, BUT THEY WERE OLDER AND I WANTED TO SEEM LIKE I WASN'T JUST A LITTLE KID, YOU KNOW?
SO I DIDN'T SAY ANYTHING.
PICK

THEY'D GO INTO MEGAMART AND GET ME A DR PEPPER LIP GLOSS AND CAN OF DR PEPPER—MY FAVORITE FLAVOR!—
AND IT MADE ME FEEL LIKE I WAS ONE OF THEM.

I DIDN'T STEAL MYSELF, SO I THOUGHT IT WAS OKAY.

BUT AFTER A BIT,

TAP TAP TAP

THEY GOT ON MY CASE ABOUT ACCEPTING STUFF WITHOUT "CONTRIBUTING."

I THINK ME NOT SHOPLIFTING MADE THEM FEEL BAD ABOUT DOING IT THEMSELVES.

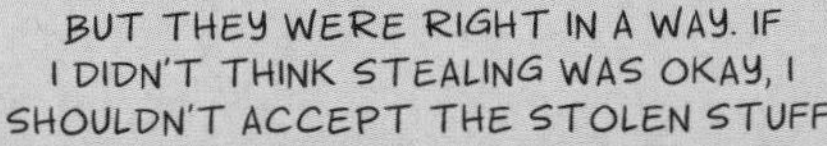

BUT THEY WERE RIGHT IN A WAY. IF I DIDN'T THINK STEALING WAS OKAY, I SHOULDN'T ACCEPT THE STOLEN STUFF.

SO WHEN WE WERE IN A BIG CORNER STORE THIS ONE DAY THAT THEY PROMISED WAS SO EASY AND NO ONE CARES, AND NO ONE EVER GETS CAUGHT HERE, I DECIDED I DID IN FACT OWE IT TO THEM.

(AND I WAS PRETTY SURE IF I DIDN'T DO IT SOON, THEY WERE GOING TO QUIT ASKING ME TO HANG OUT, WHICH SEEMED LIKE THE WORST POSSIBLE THING SOMEHOW)

SO INSTEAD OF DOING ANY OF THE OTHER THINGS I COULD HAVE DONE:

- ☐ LEAVE,

- ☐ FIND OTHER FRIENDS,
- ☐ TELL MY PARENTS,

- ☐ OR EVEN JUST MY SISTER!

I STOLE A MEGA-CHEW, IF YOU MUST KNOW, AND TWO BIG BUBS.

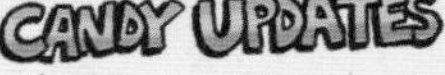

MEGA-CHEW
VERY CHEWY, TOOTH-BREAKING CARAMEL WITH CHOCOLATE AND POINTY TOFFEE PIECES. IF YOU HATE THE DENTIST: AVOID. MAY GLUE MOUTH SHUT.

MEGA-CHEW

BIG BUB REALLY BAD BUBBLE GUM. WITH REALLY CORNY COMIC STRIPS. COLLECT 1500 COMICS TO GET A SLINGSHOT. SHOOT THE GUM AT YOUR ENEMIES, KILLING THEM PROBABLY. THAT'S HOW HARD IT IS.

ALL I KNOW IS THAT THE SECOND SHE CAUGHT ME,
MEGA CHEW 2 for $.2
THEY WERE GONE.

AND THEY STAYED GONE AS THE SHOPKEEPER AND HER HUSBAND CALLED MY PARENTS.

THEY DIDN'T TEXT WHILE I WAITED FOR MY PARENTS TO PICK ME UP.

THEY DIDN'T MESSAGE ME IN ANY WAY WHEN I WAS CRYING, LISTENING TO MY PARENTS APOLOGIZE TO THE SHOPKEEPERS . . .

AND BEING **FILMED** BY SOME BRAT
WHO SOLD THE VIDEO TO CHUCK.

THE SHOPKEEPER AND HER HUSBAND OWNED THE BUSINESS THEMSELVES. THEY EVEN LIVED ABOVE IT WITH THEIR KIDS.

MOON'S

MY PARENTS MADE A DEAL WITH THEM TO HAVE ME VOLUNTEER—I WAS HAPPY TO DO IT, I FELT SO BAD. I'D CLEAN AND STOCK SHELVES AND PLAY WITH THE KIDS IN THE BACK.

EVENTUALLY THEY FORGAVE ME.

AND MY PARENTS FORGAVE ME.
I STOPPED HANGING OUT WITH THE OLDER GIRLS.
I THOUGHT IT WAS ALL OVER.

THE VIDEO WAS COMPLETE WITH DRAMATIC FREEZE-FRAMES, SOUND EFFECTS, AND HEADLINES.

WAH! WAH!

BOO HOO!

LEADERSHIP SKILLS? UP FOR DEBATE.

PRESIDENT? MORE LIKE

THIEF

STEALS FROM

SMALL, LOCAL BUSINESS!

PRESIDENT HYPOCRITE

I HAD TO HAND IT TO HIM, "PRESIDENT HYPOCRITE" COULD CATCH ON . . . IF THE VIDEO EVER GOT OUT.

DING

If you don't respond, this goes out.

DING

Tell anyone, this goes out.

DING

The whole school sees it.

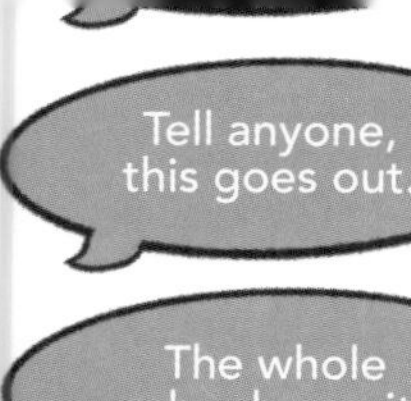
Tell anyone,
this goes out.
The whole
school sees it.
What do you want?

• • •

HE WANTED TO MEET.
HE'S GOOD.
HE DOESN'T PUT HIS NAME IN WRITING. DOESN'T DO ANYTHING THAT COULD GET HIM CAUGHT. HE DIDN'T WANT MONEY—NOT FROM ME. SOMETHING MORE COMPLICATED.
VOTE FOR HASEENA
FOR MIDDLE YEARS CLASS PRESIDENT

IT'S EASY, *PAL!*
HANG OUT WITH THE UPPER YEARS' GOVERNMENT GIRLS!

THEY'RE YOUR *FRIENDS*, AREN'T THEY?
DO WHAT YOU DO ANYWAY: HANG OUT! GRAB A SLUSHIE.

AND WHEN THEIR *STICKY FINGERS* COME OUT,

YOU TAKE THAT NEAT LITTLE PHONE OF YOURS, AND GET YOURSELF A NICE LITTLE VIDEO.
AND YOU SEND IT TO ME.

WHY?
HEH.

I'M CERTAIN THAT YOUR FRIENDS, THE *EXEMPLARY LEADERS* OF STUDENT GOVERNMENT, WILL AGREE . . .

I *DESERVE* A MORE POWERFUL VOICE AROUND HERE.

ESPECIALLY WHEN THEY SEE THE LITTLE VIDEO YOU'RE GOING TO MAKE FOR ME!

IF THEY DON'T, I THINK IT WOULD BE *TRAGIC* TO SEE SUCH A BRIGHT YOUNG STAR AS YOURSELF FALL FROM GRACE.

I DON'T THINK THE FACULTY WILL WANT A THIEVING HYPOCRITE PREACHING ABOUT SOCIAL JUSTICE LEADING THE STUDENT BODY,

DO YOU?

I KNEW I COULDN'T GO THROUGH WITH IT.
I COULDN'T TELL MY PARENTS.
WHO KNEW WHAT CHUCK WOULD DO?
AND I COULDN'T EVEN PROVE IT WAS HIM!
I BEGGED HIM FOR ANOTHER OPTION.
YAWWWNN
I'LL RAISE MONEY!
TAKE MY PHONE!
WHATEVER!
BUT NO.
THINK IT OVER, FRIENDO!
HE HAD ME.
VOTE FOR HASEENA
FOR MIDDLE YEARS CLASS PRESIDENT

SO I DID NOTHING.
HE RELEASED THE VIDEO.
ANNOUNCEMENT:
THERE HAS BEEN A CHANGE IN THE MIDDLE GRADE CABINET...
I LOST EVERYTHING.
RRIIIIIPP
BE MY VICE PREZ
CHUCK MILTON
PRESIDENT
CHUCK TOOK MY PLACE AS MIDDLE GRADE PRESIDENT.
SO HE GOT EVERYTHING HE WANTED.
Thief!
THAT'S HER.
Phony!
She stole from a family
President Hypocrite!
My parents
SCHOOL WAS MISERABLE.

MY PARENTS GOT WORRIED.

THEY WERE ON THE PHONE A LOT. I THINK WITH MY TEACHERS.

THEY SUGGESTED I CHANGE TO THE OTHER SCHOOL IN THE DISTRICT.

I AGREED.

AFTER HOLIDAY BREAK, I DIDN'T GO BACK.

Chapter 13

AT THE NEW SCHOOL, I CHANGED MY LOOK. I FOCUSED ON SPORTS.
BASKETBALL TRYOUTS
BOYS GIRLS
I DID TRACK,
VOLLEYBALL,
BADMINTON . . .
BUT I LIKED BASKETBALL THE BEST.
ALL POSTS MUST BE APPROVED BY COMMUNITY CENTRE ADMIN.
COMMUNITY RECREATION BASKETBALL
3-5 6-8 9-12
16-18 ADULT
LEARN GUITAR
THE CRAFT
SCREENING
STORY TIME
JCC TALK SERIE
I LIKED IT SO MUCH THAT THIS YEAR I JOINED THE COMMUNITY LEAGUE.
BASKETBALL
3-5 6-8 9-12
13-15 16-18 ADULT
DOWNSIDE: THE REC CENTER WHERE THEY PRACTICED WAS REALLY CLOSE TO MY OLD SCHOOL. HIGH CROSS-OVER RISK. I WANTED TO STAY ANONYMOUS.

UPSIDE: IT TURNED OUT THE ONLY KID FROM MY OLD SCHOOL WAS A NEW GIRL WHO DIDN'T KNOW A THING ABOUT MY PAST.
SO I DIDN'T TELL YOU.
SORRY.
IT'S OKAY. I UNDERSTAND. ACTUALLY . . .
I HAVE SOMETHING TO TELL YOU TOO.
ME AND SHIRLEY?
OUR PARENTS DON'T MAKE US PLAY.
SHE'S MY REAL FRIEND.
OH.

I KNOW SHE'S PRETTY DIFFERENT,
BUT WHEN YOU GET TO KNOW HER, SHE'S REALLY FUN AND SMART.
SHE'S SORT OF MY *FIRST* REAL FRIEND.

WHY DIDN'T YOU SAY?

UM.
BECAUSE YOU'RE MY SECOND REAL FRIEND. I THOUGHT YOU DIDN'T LIKE HER.

SHE'S PRETTY WEI—
DON'T SAY WEIRD.

UNUSUAL.
BUT IF YOU LIKE HER, SHE'S PROBABLY OKAY.

I DON'T KNOW IF YOU'LL GET ALONG.
WHO CARES!

YOUR FRIENDS DON'T ALL HAVE TO BE FRIENDS WITH EACH OTHER!

$xy=ab^2$
$e=mc^2$

THEY DON'T?
NO WAY! WHEN I WENT HERE I HAD DEBATE FRIENDS, STUDENT GOVERNMENT FRIENDS, LUNCH CLUB FRIENDS . . . SOME OF THEM COULDN'T STAND EACH OTHER!

BUT SHIRLEY AND I ALREADY HAVE SOMETHING IN COMMON.
WHAT'S THAT?
WE BOTH LIKE YOU.

SPEAKING OF SHIRLEY...
YEAH?

SHE NEVER TOLD YOU WHO I WAS?
SHE KNEW?!

OF COURSE! YOU BOTH WENT HERE!

SHE NEVER SAID ANYTHING TO ME! DID SHE KNOW THIS WHOLE TIME?
THIS IS THE QUESTION.

HEY.

SPEAKING OF SHIRLEY AGAIN...
ISN'T THAT HER?
OH YEAH! SHE SAID SHE MIGHT COME BY.

YOU TWO HAVE ONE OTHER THING IN COMMON, BESIDES ME.
YEAH?

YOU'RE BOTH GOOD AT STEALING FROM CHUCK MILTON AND GETTING AWAY WITH IT.

SHIRLEY AND I EXPLAINED THE WHOLE THING TO SEENA. CHUCK, THE SNEAKING IN, EVERYTHING.

I DON'T THINK SHE CLOSED HER MOUTH THE WHOLE TIME.

WHEN IT WAS OVER, I WAITED FOR HER TO SAY SOMETHING.

YOU WERE BOTH THERE?
UH-HUH.
YOU HEARD EVERYTHING.
WE DIDN'T MEAN TO.
THAT'S AMAZING!
SHIRLEY, DID YOU KNOW WHO SEENA WAS THE WHOLE TIME?
YEAH! WHEN YOU RAN UP AFTER PRACTICE THAT TIME, I WAS SWEATING!
IT HELPED THAT YOU TOTALLY IGNORED ME.
MY APOLOGIES.
I'VE BEEN TOLD I CAN OVER-FOCUS, OFTEN TO THE DETRIMENT OF,
UM, SOCIAL NICETIES.

I DIDN'T MAKE THE CONNECTION AT FIRST. IN FACT IT WAS ONLY IN CHUCK'S BEDROOM THAT I PUT THE PIECES TOGETHER.
THEN I THOUGHT JAMILA WOULD LIKE TO FIGURE IT OUT ON HER OWN.
IT WAS YOUR IDEA TO BREAK INTO CHUCK'S?

IT WAS.

SHE HAD TO CONVINCE ME TO *FLOUT THE LAW.* I'M REAL GLAD SHE DID.
SAME.

YOU KNOW, I THINK WE'RE GOING TO GET ALONG FINE.

Chapter 14

WE WOUND UP GIVING SEENA EVERYTHING WE GOT FROM CHUCK'S.
I DON'T KNOW WHAT I'M GONNA DO WITH THIS YET.
IF YOU FIGURE IT OUT AND NEED HELP . . .
INDEED!

IT TOOK HER A WHILE.

!
I GOT IT!

ABOUT A WEEK LATER:
LOOKS LIKE SEENA DECIDED.
SHE SURE DID.

HAVE **YOU** BEEN BLACKMAILED

by CHUCK MILTON?

WE HAVE TOO.

NEVER FEAR: WE HAVE YOUR STUFF!!

EVERY
★ NOTE
★ VIDEO
★ BIT OF DIRT

HAS BEEN RECLAIMED.

GO TO BadLuckChuck.ca

IDENTIFY WHAT HE STOLE FROM YOU

WE BURN -OR- RETURN THE DIRT!

This is REAL, PEOPLE.

CHUCK IS **OVER.**

WOW.

WON'T CHILDREN BE SUSPICIOUS THAT THIS IS CHUCK, TRYING TO GET IT ALL BACK? OR SOME NEW KIDS TRYING TO TAKE HIS POWER?
SEENA RECRUITED OTHER KNOWN SURVIVORS OF CHUCK'S—KIDS WHOSE SECRETS WERE ALREADY OUT BECAUSE THEY'D FAILED TO PAY UP.

SHE GAVE THEM BACK THEIR ORIGINAL DOCUMENTS.

THEY ALL WEIGHED IN ON WHAT TO DO WITH THE REST.

THEY'RE SPREADING THE WORD TOGETHER.

AFTER TWO RECESSES,

EVERYONE WILL KNOW.

BY LUNCHTIME **EVERYONE** KNEW CHUCK'S POWER GRAB WAS OVER, AND THE WEBSITE WAS LEGIT.

BY THE END OF THE DAY, WELL . . .
RAAAAAAA

SORRY, CHUCK!
YOU CAN'T KICK ME OUT! I KNOW ALL ABOUT—
Student council meets TODAY

ABOUT WHAT, CHUCK?

"SHOPLIFTING"? YOU LOST YOUR PROOF! PLUS MY PARENTS KNOW NOW. I'VE GOT NOTHING TO HIDE.
LOOKS LIKE SEENA WASN'T THE ONLY PERSON HE BLACKMAILED TO GET THERE.

SLAM

IT'S NOT **FAIR**! YOU CAN'T! I **DESERVE** TO BE HERE! BECAUSE . . . BECAUSE . . .
THAT IS NOT A WELL-RESEARCHED ARGUMENT, CHUCK.
BUT YOU'RE SWEET! GOOD LUCK!
Student council meets TODAY

AAAAAAAAAAAAAAAAA
SLAM
I WISH I COULD SAY CHUCK TOOK SEENA'S ADVICE AND MADE SOME REAL FRIENDS. BUT THAT'S HARD WHEN YOU'RE USED TO BEING THE BOSS ALL THE TIME.
I HOPE HE CAN.
FRIENDS MAKE ALL THE DIFFERENCE.
DO YOU WANT TO COME OVER?
UH-HUH.

I SAID WE'D WALK PART WAY WITH—
HERE SHE IS!
HEY!

FANTASTIC!

IN THE MEANTIME, TELL ME **EVERYTHING.**
30
CASE CLOSED